INDIANA JONES

and the
TEMPLE OF DOOM

Suzanne Weyn

Based on the story by George Lucas and Philip Kaufman,
and the screenplay by Willard Huyck & Gloria Katz

Scholastic Inc.

New York   Toronto   London   Auckland   Sydney
Mexico City   New Delhi   Hong Kong   Buenos Aires

ISBN-13: 978-0-545-04255-0
ISBN-10: 0-545-04255-0

12 11 10 9 8 7 6 5 4 3 2   8 9 10 11 12/0

Designed by Rick DeMonico
Printed in the U.S.A.
First printing, April 2008

INDIANA JONES ™

and the
TEMPLE OF DOOM

Princeton University, 1935

Indiana Jones, professor of anthropology, known to his friends and enemies alike by his nickname, Indy, walked into his father's office in the medieval division of the history department at Princeton University. He put down the battered satchel that carried his traveling clothes.

He settled into a high-back leather chair to wait for his father, Dr. Henry Jones, Sr. As he stretched out, he sighed contentedly.

Indiana Jones was no stranger to worldwide travel. In fact he'd spent most of his life traipsing around the globe, first as a boy accompanying his parents on the many lecture tours his scholarly father gave in various countries, later as a young Allied soldier and spy during World War I. And these days he traveled in his role as a professor of archaeology. He participated in only the most fascinating digs for ancient treasure, and sometimes sought these treasures for private collectors.

He rose from the chair and paced around the office. Where was his father? Indy couldn't stand waiting. He was restless and impatient by nature. It was the reason he could never settle down to the safe life of a full-time professor at a university, despite his vast knowledge of the exotic, strange treasures of the ancient world. Usually, he'd teach for a few semesters — he was both a professor of archaeology and linguistics, specializing in ancient tongues — and then things would seem too quiet, even boring, and he'd yearn for a new adventure.

Still ... the adventurous life could be exhausting. It was certainly dangerous. He was looking forward to a little rest and relaxation now.

He glanced fretfully at his watch. It annoyed him to sit around doing nothing.

He'd taken a chance on catching his father between classes. But obviously, he'd diverted from his usual schedule, perhaps he'd taken a meeting or left to attend a colleague's lecture. Indy knew he could be waiting a while. Luckily, there was always something interesting to read in his father's office. He glanced around the room, checking out the books and manuscripts: the older, the better.

But on his father's wide desk, he spotted something decidedly modern. It was a pile of unopened mail — his mail. Indy had almost forgotten his request that the post office forward everything to his father while he was in the South Pacific. He checked the stack and, sure enough, all the letters were addressed to him.

Well, it wouldn't be as interesting as leafing through an old text, but as long as he was waiting, Indy figured he might as well do something useful. He began to sort through the various correspondences. Bills. Bills. Some scholarly journals, one of which contained an article he had written on ancient Chinese artifacts of the Tsang Dynasty. It was a subject that had come to fascinate him lately.

He came to a letter that particularly intrigued him and he put the others back on the desk. Its foreign stamps, postmark, and return address indicated that it had come from Shanghai, China.

He had a number of friends and acquaintants in Shanghai; one of his closest associates was a man named Wu Han, with whom he'd worked on various archae-ological adventures. But he didn't recognize the writing as belonging to any of the people he knew.

Burning with curiosity, he tore open the letter. *Dr. Jones,* it began. *Your reputation is known to us. We require your services. We are in possession of the Eye of the Peacock, which we offer to you as payment, though you must promise not to inquire how we came to possess such a prize. If these terms are agreeable to you, be at the observation deck of the Empire State Building at sundown on July 6.* The letter ended there with no signature.

The Eye of the Peacock! He'd come so close to obtaining the magnificent diamond years ago, only to have it slip through his fingers. Was it possible that this collector really had it in his possession — and, if he did have it, that he was willing to part with it? It sounded too incredible to be true.

Who could possess this mythical diamond without the world knowing about it? It had to be owned by some sort of underworld black-market dealer in antiquities, a thief, or a mobster of some kind.

It would be safer to steer clear of having someone like that as an employer. Who knew what kind of danger it could lead to?

And yet . . . if it was *true*, how could he pass up the chance to actually get his hands on the Eye of the Peacock diamond? It was a rare treasure that the entire world had the right to see.

He glanced at the calendar on his father's wall. July 6 was today! If he left immediately, he could get to the Empire State Building by sundown.

Snapping up his satchel and leaving the rest of his unopened mail behind, he was quickly out the door.

CHAPTER ONE

Shanghai, China, December 1935

Indiana Jones stopped at the top of the stairs and peered down at the elegantly dressed patrons of the opulent, art-deco style Obi Wan night club. The international assortment of lavishly coiffed women wore glittering evening gowns and their equally intercontinental partners were in black tuxedos from the city's finest tailors.

Indy was dressed to fit right in, decked out in his new white tuxedo jacket with contrasting black pants and vest. The Shanghai tailor who had sold it to him had said that this year everyone would be wearing this style. "It's the latest from Paris," he'd insisted. "For 1935, it is the style to have."

Since coming to China months earlier, he hadn't worn his trademark leather jacket and snap-brim hat much. There had been little need to dress for action. Most of his digging had been through the dusty back rooms of Chinese museums and the musty, crumbling scrolls of antique archives. Except for a mercilessly bouncy yak ride over the Himalayas where he and his companions Wu Han and Short Round had been beset by nomadic thieves and the relatively minor matter of having to escape from a band of mountain-dwelling rogue monks who had tried to imprison him . . . it had been a fairly uneventful time.

Indiana spotted the stylishly dressed men he'd come to meet sitting together at a table not far from the stage. They were Shanghai's notorious crime boss Lao Che and his two thuggish sons, Chen and Kao Kan.

Lao Che turned out to be the "private collector of valuable antiquities" who had written to him. Just as Indy had guessed, he was one of Shanghai's most notorious crime lords. Undoubtedly, he had come into possession of the Eye of the Peacock Diamond through underhanded means, but he had not asked Indy to do anything illegal. And now Indiana felt he would be undoing any wrong Lao Che might have done by bringing the diamond to a world-class museum. He would charge a fee, of course, but it would only be fair considering all the work he'd done to bring this spectacular diamond to the world.

Lao Che and his sons didn't notice Indy because they were watching the show on the stage with rapt attention. Following the intent focus of their gazes, Indy surveyed the act. A beautiful blond singer wore a red gown covered in shimmering beads that sparkled with her every flowing gesture. She glided across the stage crooning Cole Porter's latest hit, "Anything Goes," in what Indy considered to be pretty good Mandarin. It would be tempting to let this bedazzling singer hypnotize him with her violet blue eyes, blond curls, and a voice like liquid gold, but he had other things on his mind at the moment.

At the bottom of the stairs, Indy's friend and helper, Wu Han, crossed in front of him disguised as a waiter. "Be careful," he murmured under his breath so that only Indy could hear him.

Wu Han was there as backup in case the deal between Lao Che and Indy turned nasty. They already had good reason to believe that it would. In the months since Indy had been in China, he'd seen how the crime chief operated, and Indy fully expected that Lao Che would soon be up to his old tricks.

Indy had done some planning, just in case his worst fears were realized. Wu Han and Indy's junior assistant, Short Round, would be there to help if things went south. They had worked out a course of action in scrupulous detail. With this plan in place, Indy was reasonably sure that he'd make it out of there — even if things went terribly wrong.

Crossing the crowded club filled with tables of rambunctious, fun-loving patrons who watched the show while they popped champagne corks, Indy took a seat at the table across from Lao Che and his sons. He greeted them in Shanghainese, one of the Chinese Wu dialects he spoke fluently. While he talked, two of Lao Che's men frisked him for any concealed weapons but found none.

"You never told me you spoke my language, Dr. Jones," Lao Che commented.

"Only on special occasions," Indy replied politely. This wasn't entirely true. He often spoke the dialect most used in Shanghai whenever he was in the city. But he wanted to underscore the fact that tonight was a momentous occasion. It was the end of the line, the final moment in the undertaking that had brought him halfway around the world.

"So, is it true, you found the Nurhachi?" Lao Che inquired, a bright eagerness coming to his dark eyes. He leaned forward attentively, barely controlling his excitement.

A sneer curled Indy's lip. "You *know* I did," he responded disdainfully. His eyes bore into those of Lao Che's son, Chen. "Last night one of your *boys* tried to get Nurhachi without paying for him."

Chen lowered his bandaged hand below the table and glowered at Indy. Just the night before, he had broken into Indy's apartment with three other of Lao Che's thugs and tried to steal the Nurhachi, the prize Lao Che had commissioned Indy to procure. Indy had suspected that Lao

Che would try something like this and was ready for them. He'd broken Chen's hand as he twisted the gun away from him. It was one of the reasons he'd asked Wu Han to watch his back tonight.

"You have insulted my son," Lao Che barked angrily.

Indy kept cool. "No, *you* have insulted *me*," he insisted levelly. "*I* spared *his* life."

Lao Che's other son, Kao Kan, rose from the table, cursing in Chinese, ready to spring at Indy. Lao Che motioned for him to sit.

Indy kept his eyes on the three crime lords sitting across the table from him. He was dimly aware that the blond singer from the stage show had come to the table, but this was no time to let himself become distracted.

She draped her red satin, elbow-length gloved hand over Lao Che's shoulder. "Aren't you going to introduce us?" she asked Lao Che. Her voice was warm and flirtatious. From her accent, he placed her as being decidedly Midwestern American.

Lao Che kept his eyes on Indy as he spoke. "This is Willie Scott," he said with the slightest nod toward the woman at his shoulder. "This is Indiana Jones, the famous archaeologist."

Willie smiled and her pearly teeth shone between her shining red lips. She slid into a seat between Indy and Lao Che.

Excellent, Indy thought, adjusting his plan to suit the new development. She was exactly where he wanted her.

"Well," Willie said smoothly, looking him over appreciatively. "I thought archaeologists were always funny little men searching for their mommies."

"You mean, *mummies*," Indiana corrected, not sure if she had been joking.

He assessed her quickly, not letting his eyes wander from his adversaries for more than seconds at a time. Under all that exotic makeup and the slinky dress, she was a classic American beauty. She must have seen some rough times to have landed in Shanghai, singing in a nightclub, the moll of an unscrupulous crime lord like Lao Che. He wondered what unfortunate circumstances had brought her here.

"Dr. Jones found Nurhachi for me," Lao Che explained to Willie. "And he's going to deliver him . . . now!"

Indy was aware that Kao Kan was holding a pistol under the table and aiming it right at him.

"Say, who is this Nurhachi?" Willie asked.

Before anyone could answer her question, Indiana pulled Willie over to him, grabbed a carving fork from a nearby tray and jabbed it into her side. She tried to squirm away from him, her eyes wide with fright, but he had a firm hold on her waist and pulled her closer.

It was exactly what he'd been planning since he realized Kao Kan was holding a gun on him. The moment Willie had sat beside him, Indy saw the chance to turn the tables. "Put the gun away, sonny," he growled at Kao Kan.

Kao Kan looked to his father uncertainly. Lao Che nodded for him to put the gun away.

Indiana kept his hold on Willie, but took the fork from her side. He didn't really want to hurt her, but he'd had to make it look real. For that to happen, Lao Che had to see true fear on her face. "Now I suggest you give me what you owe me, or anything goes," he threatened.

Around them, the patrons of the club were still unaware of the scene unfolding at Lao Che's table. They popped more champagne corks and laughed, oblivious to the explosive situation threatening to erupt in their midst.

Beside him, Willie whimpered and gazed at Lao Che, silently, her eyes imploring him to hand over Indiana's payment so he would release her. At a signal from his father, Chen reached into his pocket and set a small, velvet pouch on the revolving tray at the table's center and spun it toward Indy.

As the pouch swung into position in front of him, Indy could feel his excitement growing. The diamond was so close he could touch it! But he controlled himself, refusing to touch the pouch. Who knew what trap they had set for him?

He nudged Willie closer to the table. "Open it," he demanded gruffly.

With trembling hands, she poured ten gold coins onto the revolving tray. Only ten gold coins! He should have known this would happen!

"The diamond, Lao," Indiana snarled, enraged but not surprised. "The deal was for the diamond!"

He wouldn't have gone through all the difficulty of getting Nurhachi, wouldn't have dealt with Lao Che at all, if he hadn't been promised the enormous Eye of the Peacock.

Lao Che reached into his pocket and placed another pouch on the revolving tray beside a glass of champagne. Grunting unhappily, he spun it over to Indiana.

Once again, Indy nudged Willie to open the pouch. Her eyes widened and his mouth was agape at the sight of the spectacularly brilliant, luminous diamond inside. It was priceless: larger than a walnut and beautifully cut. "Oh, Lao," she murmured, awestruck. Sighing, she wrapped her fingers around it possessively.

Indy jabbed her once again with the carving fork, this time harder than before. A short, sharp, high-pitched shriek erupted from her lips.

Scowling fiercely at him, she released the diamond into his outstretched palm.

Indiana smiled. The job was over and everything had come off as he'd hoped. He lifted the champagne from the tray, relieved.

He'd left his junior assistant, Short Round, with instructions to book all three of them on a flight to Bangkok that very night. In a half hour, Short Round would come to collect Wu Han and Indy to drive them all to the airfield.

From Bangkok, they would fly to London. He'd already contacted a colleague at the British Museum who had expressed great interest in obtaining the diamond for their Far East exhibit. *Maybe I'll visit friends at London University,* he thought, twirling the stem of the champagne glass in his fingers, but not drinking. He had taught at London University for a time and had enjoyed it very much.

Yes, life was looking good. "To your very good health," he toasted Lao Che, raising his glass and feeling very pleased indeed.

He released his hold on Willie's waist, and she instantly leaped away from him. "Lao," she shouted angrily, "he put a hole ... he put two holes in my dress from Paris!"

Indy tensed. How much did Willie Scott mean to Lao

Che? Would he retaliate if his girlfriend insisted on it? Was he in for more trouble?

"Sit down!" Lao Che barked at her and Indy relaxed once again. Willie Scott would not be a threat to him.

Willie plunked back down into her seat, but slid her chair well out of Indy's reach. She wasn't stupid and clearly had no intention of becoming his hostage again.

"Now you bring me Nurhachi," Lao Che demanded smoothly.

Indy grinned at him and nodded. "My pleasure." He beckoned to Wu Han, who lingered nearby, still pretending to be a waiter.

"Who on earth is this Nurhachi?" Willie asked, bewildered and aggravated at being kept in the dark.

Before anyone could answer her, Wu Han approached and presented a tray. On it was a six-inch high carved jade urn. Indy placed the urn on the table's revolving tray, turning it toward Lao Che. "Here he is," he announced.

Willie turned to Lao, still completely puzzled. "This Nurhachi is a real small guy," she remarked, her brow creasing in confusion.

"Inside are the ashes of Nurhachi, the first emperor of the Manchu Dynasty," Lao Che explained solemnly. He lifted the urn with two hands, turning it reverently.

Indy sat drinking his champagne and watching Lao Che. Having this dead emperor's ashes obviously meant a lot to him. *Strange*, he thought. Did owning an emperor make him feel important — like he was also an emperor, too, ruler of his own crime-infested world? Possibly.

Whatever Lao Che's reasons were, Indy had to admit, at least to himself, that he'd enjoyed the challenge of finding the urn containing Nurhachi's ashes. Years earlier, it had been smuggled out of China and sold on the black market. Through rigorous research and with steely determination, Indy had tracked the urn to a tiny, dark pawn shop in Istanbul where it had been sitting unopened for years.

Indiana toasted Nurhachi. "Welcome home, old boy," he said, draining the last drops from his glass.

Lao Che, Chen, and Kao Kan began to chuckle giddily with delight. "And now give the diamond back to me," Lao Che said.

It was Indy's turn to be puzzled. "Are you trying to develop a sense of humor or am I going deaf?" he asked. Surely he hadn't heard Lao Che correctly. The man couldn't be serious!

Indy squirmed uncomfortably in his chair, though he tried to hide it. He didn't like being the only one not in on their little joke. It didn't seem to him that these guys had much of a sense of humor. The only kind of joke they would find this funny was one in which the joke was on him.

The three men broke into gales of even more uproarious

laughter, practically falling off their chairs as they convulsed. Kao Kan pounded the table. Chen could barely breathe and clutched his sides as his shoulders shook with merriment.

Suddenly the smile faded from Lao Che's face. He held up a vial of vivid blue liquid.

"What's that?" Indy asked.

"Antidote," Lao Che replied, suddenly quite serious.

Indy didn't like the sound of that. "To what?"

"The poison you just drank, Dr. Jones," he said.

Indy swirled his finger around the inside of the champagne glass. It came out covered in a filmy, white residue. There had indeed been something more than champagne in his glass. Indy cursed his carelessness: He should have expected something like this.

Swallowing, he realized he was suddenly nauseated and his throat was swelling. He'd begun to sweat, and his hands had picked up a slight but uncontrollable tremor. This wasn't fear — it was the poison taking effect.

Lao Che smirked at him. "The poison works fast, Dr. Jones," he said, deadly serious now.

Indy knew he had to hold on somehow and stay as calm as possible. He couldn't afford to have his heart rate get any faster. It would only send the poison coursing through his bloodstream with greater speed. If he was going to get out of this on the winning end, he had to think quickly and not let the poison take him down.

The time to act was now — while he still could.

Willie squealed as he lunged for her. Digging her high heels into the floor, she tried to slide away from him, but her chair tipped almost spilling her onto the floor. Once again, he grabbed her waist and jabbed the fork into her side.

"Lao!" she shouted.

"Lao . . ." Indy growled at the same time, his voice overlapping Willie's.

He didn't really want to hurt Willie, but he hoped Lao Che didn't know that. Indy just hoped he cared enough to save her.

Unfortunately, Lao Che was unfazed. "You keep the girl," he said. "I'll find another."

The room seemed to be spinning and the voices all around became garbled. This was bad. How much longer could Indy hold himself together? He might not have much time left. He had to force himself to think clearly.

Letting go of Willie, Indy shook his head, breathed deeply, and felt his mind clear slightly. Scanning the room, he was relieved to find Wu Han among the crowd. With a wave of his hand, he signaled his friend.

Wu Han arrived at the table holding a drained

champagne glass on the same silver tray he had brought Nurhachi on earlier. This time, though, he raised it ever-so-slightly to reveal that it concealed the pistol he was aiming at Lao Che.

Indy smiled at Wu Han. "Good service here," he remarked with a grin. With Wu Han by his side, armed, things were looking a lot less hopeless.

"That's not a waiter!" Willie gasped.

"Wu Han's an old friend," Indy told her. Wu Han nodded at him confidently, keeping the three mobsters in his steely sight. Indy knew Wu Han was an excellent shot.

"Game's over, Lao," Indy said, rising as best he could from the table.

All around them, patrons continued to laugh and open champagne bottles which popped loudly when the corks were pulled. The pops masked the shot when Kao Kan fired his pistol at Wu Han.

A look of profound puzzlement swept over Wu Han's face. At first, he didn't even understand what had happened. He saw the shattered glass on his tray and then noticed the red bloodstain slowly spreading across his white shirt. Moments later, the pain registered with him. "Indy!" he cried, clutching his chest.

Indy grabbed hold of Wu Han, easing him onto a chair at the table. He hadn't heard the shot, either. It took his clouded mind a minute to realize what had happened to his friend.

Looking around, he saw that the muffled shooting had still not attracted any attention and the nightclub's activity was continuing as usual. It gave the situation an air of unreality. How could this be happening in the middle of all these people with no one noticing?

"Don't worry, Wu Han," Indy said to his friend. "I'll get you out of here." No matter how badly the poison was affecting him, he had to come through. If he had to crawl out, dragging Wu Han behind him, he would do it.

Wu Han gazed up at Indy, his visage pale with pain, his voice fading. "Not this time, Indy," he said, smiling bravely even though his eyes were rapidly clouding over. "I've followed you on many adventures, but into the great Unknown Mystery, I go first, Indy." He'd barely gotten the words out when he slumped to the table.

Indy lunged forward to feel Wu Han's pulse — but found none. No! It couldn't be! When he'd asked Wu Han to back him up, he knew there might be trouble, but he never expected his friend to end up dead.

"Don't be sad, Dr. Jones," Lao Che sneered. "You will soon be joining him."

CHAPTER TWO

Stunned with grief, Indy's gaze drifted over to Lao Che's smirking face. Beside him, Chen continued to giggle and the murderous Kao Kan gloated triumphantly.

Indy burned with rage. Normally he would have tried to avenge Wu Han's murder, but the room was lurching erratically now as the poison continued to course through his veins.

Impulsively, he staggered angrily toward Lao Che, but was thrown off balance by the affects of the poison. He gripped the table for support.

"Too much to drink, Dr. Jones?" Lao Che taunted.

Summoning all his energy, Indy righted himself but then stumbled backward as the room spun yet again. He collided with a waiter who had just set a row of Cognac-soaked skewered pigeons on fire at a nearby table.

The dish was a delicacy, a specialty of Club Obi Wan, but to Indy it was something else — a weapon. Grabbing one skewer, he hurled the long spear of flaming pigeons at Kao Kan.

At the same moment, Kao Kan fired at Indy, but missed. He screamed as the flaming, improvised spear pierced his chest.

This — a man being wounded with a flaming row of cooked birds — was finally something the other patrons of the club could not miss!

Screams erupted.

People leaped to their feet and began to flee the club in terror.

Lao Che bolted up, bellowing threats at Indy in Chinese. Indy threw himself across the table with abandon, desperate to get hold of the vial of antidote in Lao Che's hand.

Willie stood nearby, now holding the diamond. When Indy charged past, the diamond was knocked from her hand! It slid across the floor into the crowd of panicked, escaping patrons, stampeding for the nearest door. With a cry of anguished disappointment, Willie plunged into the onrushing crowd—and risked being trampled — to retrieve the fabulous gem.

Lao Che sprang away as Indiana barreled into him, grabbing for his wrist. In the struggle, the vial flew into the air and was soon sliding and being kicked across the room along with the diamond.

Indy crawled across the floor after the spinning vial — the diamond could wait. If he didn't get the vial, though, it would probably mean the final end of all his adventures. He'd encountered various poisons in his travels but never one this fast-acting or potent.

The nightclub was in an uproar as people trampled one another, pushing and shoving to get out. The rolling vial was kicked underfoot, making it impossible for Indy to get hold of it. Several times it was almost in reach when it was knocked across the room by a stampeding patron.

As Indy crawled across the floor, he saw that Willie was also on her hands and knees, pursuing the diamond. If she got hold of it, she would probably disappear with the fortune it would bring. For a moment, he considered going after her to be sure she wouldn't run off with his payment. He couldn't though. All his remaining energy had to be spent getting that vial before it was too late.

Unaware of the scene going on in the audience, a line of tapping show girls began to dance onto the stage, beginning the next show. At the same time, Lao Che's army of tuxedo-wearing hoods raced into the club. The chorus girls screamed and fled the stage when they saw them.

Lao Che barked orders at his men in Chinese. Reaching into their formal jackets, they produced small but deadly sharp axes. And they didn't pause before hurling them all in Indy's direction. He lunged for cover behind a life-sized female statue near the stage, but now he was trapped there as the axes whizzed past the statue or bounced off of it.

He saw that Willie was still out crawling on the floor, seemingly oblivious to the flying axes. She cursed and stomped the floor with her delicate fists as buckets of ice on stands were accidentally toppled, sending cubes everywhere and making it nearly impossible to find the diamond among them.

Indy continued watching from behind the statue and noticed Willie reaching out for the vial of antidote that came skidding past her through the ice. Its blue liquid sparkled. She plucked it up and tucked it into the bodice of her gown.

That was good. She would certainly be easier to keep in sight than a little vial of blue liquid.

Now all he had to do was find a way to get to Willie Scott!

CHAPTER THREE

*I*ndy jumped out from behind the statue, ducking and covering his head to avoid the flying axes. In the confusion, someone released hundreds of balloons that had been bound up in nets in the ceiling.

The sea of bouncing balloons covered everything, making it impossible to avoid the ice cubes on the floor. Everyone began sliding, colliding with furniture, and crashing into each other.

Darting and weaving through the crowd and Lao Che's henchmen, Indy didn't know how much longer he could last. Passing an abandoned glass of champagne, he threw it in his own face just to keep from passing out.

Before Indy could reach Willie, Chen spotted him. He snapped up a machine gun and began firing, not caring that he was shooting into the crowd.

As bullets sprayed around him, Indy sailed across the room, throwing himself behind an immense, round, brass gong for cover. Darting out just long enough to grab a large broadsword from the hands of a nearby warrior statue, he brought the sword down on the cords that fastened the huge gong to its stand.

The immense gong bounced from its stand.

C-r-r-as-s-sh!

It hit the floor and began to roll across the room on its side.

Indy ran along behind it, using the gong as a moving shield as Chen continued to fire at him. The rapid-fire bullets ricocheted from the gong, clanging ceaselessly as the huge metal disc rolled across the room, gaining momentum and traveling ever faster.

Peeking around the side of the gong, Indy observed Willie heading for an exit. Her eyes widened in terror when she turned to see the gigantic gong rolling toward her.

Indy reached out and once again wrapped his arms around her waist, pulling her to him. "Come on," he yelled. He knew she had the antidote, which meant he couldn't let her out of his sight.

"I don't want to go!" she shrieked. She demanded in loud tones that Indy release her as he pulled her along behind the gong toward a tall, stained-glass floor-to-ceiling window. Indy anxiously tightened his hold on her waist.

The gong was about to crash through the third story

window and they would have no choice but to go out with it!

"One ... two ... three ..." he counted down.

Willie clung to him, screaming wildly as they smashed through the window with the gong, their bodies plummeting into the night.

The gong flew away from them, spinning off into the darkness. They hurtled downward, shouting in terror, their arms and legs flailing wildly.

At the second floor they crashed through an open awning with a deafening ripping sound of torn fabric assailing their ears.

Landing hard on the first-story awning, they bounced up and came down again near the awning's edge. Another bounce would send them pounding down onto the pavement below.

Before that could happen, Indy hooked his foot onto the edge of the awning and grabbed hold of Willie, pulling her back down. They slid along the awning for several feet, but were both able to grip the rim and hold tight.

Willie and Indy hung there, their feet dangling six feet above the ground. "Who *are* you?" Willie asked, panting breathlessly, amazed at what had just happened. Indy wanted to grin and say something witty in reply, but his head was more clouded than ever and bouncing out a third story window hadn't helped any.

In the next second, a canvas-topped car careened around the corner of the neon-lit street below them. It was a car Indy couldn't have been happier to see.

"Jump," he told Willie as he let go. She also released her hold on the awning rim and the two of them fell, tearing through the car's roof and landing in the car's spacious backseat.

Behind the wheel was an eleven-year-old Chinese boy, a street urchin named Short Round, Indiana's bodyguard and junior assistant. "Wow! Holy smoke!" he cried. "Crash landing!"

"For cryin' out loud, there's a kid driving the car!" Willie cried when she got a good look at Short Round and realized how young he was.

"Short Round, step on it!" Indy instructed urgently. He tried to calculate how long it would take Lao Che's men to scramble down three flights of stairs. In his current blurry-headed state, he couldn't do the math, but he knew they'd be right behind.

"Okey, dokey, Dr. Jones," Short Round replied.

A block of wood strapped to his feet enabled Short Round to reach the car's pedals. With a no-nonsense scowl, he yanked the bill of his New York Yankees baseball cap to the back, hunched forward, and stomped down on the gas pedal. "Hold onto your potatoes," he shouted gleefully, zooming off.

The car's tires squealed. Willie and Indy were thrown abruptly back against the seat. "Oh!" Willie cried in distressed surprise as her head hit the seat hard.

The car raced past the entrance to Club Obi Wan just as Lao Che and his thug army raced out. Lao Che instantly recognized Indy's car and ordered his men to chase after it. The armed thugs piled into a black sedan and revved the engine. Peeling out into the crowded Shanghai street, they zoomed off after Indy, Short Round, and Willie.

As Short Round drove faster and faster to escape the sedan, Indy knew he didn't have much time left. "Where's the antidote?" he asked Willie urgently.

She batted her eyes at him, feigning bewilderment. He didn't have time for this little game! He asked again and when she didn't answer, he lunged at her. "Let me have it," he shouted, shaking her.

"Ohhh, I hope you choke," she snarled, handing the vial to him.

Indy didn't waste a second. Throwing away the stopper, he guzzled down the blue liquid. He hoped it was the real thing and not another one of Lao Che's double crosses.

"Hey, Dr. Jones, we've got company," Short Round informed him as gunfire shattered the rear window glass.

Willie ducked, terrified in the back corner of the seat. "No shooting!" she insisted.

Indy ignored her and shot back at their pursuing attackers through the broken back window while Short Round continued his lunatic drive through the crowded streets. After several rounds of gunfire, Indy needed to reload. He handed his gun to Willie while he went for the bullets he knew were in the glove compartment.

The gun was red hot. Willie juggled it, tossing the searing metal from one hand to the other. Finally, she couldn't stand it any longer. Not knowing what to do with it, exactly, she tossed the gun out the window. At the same moment, Indy reached out for her to hand the gun to him.

When he turned back to find out why she wasn't giving him the gun, he saw that it was gone. "Where's my gun?" he shouted. "Where's my gun?"

"I burnt my fingers and I cracked a nail," she whined.

Indy fought down the anger rising inside him. He could see that Willie Scott was going to be no help to him whatsoever.

Finally, Short Round screeched onto an airfield on the outskirts of Shanghai. He wheeled the car past a small terminal and proceeded to the cargo area.

Out on the field, a tri-motor plane revved its engines. The car squealed to a stop and Indy leaped out, followed by Willie. Short Round caught up to them, carrying the knapsack packed with a few essentials they'd need for the trip ahead.

At the boarding gate, a very proper airline official ran out to meet them. "Ah, Dr. Jones," he greeted Indy in a clipped British accent. "I'm, ah, Weber. I spoke with your . . . uh . . . *assistant*," he added, glancing at Short Round curiously, slowly realizing he had been talking to this child.

Short Round simply nodded seriously, silently acknowledging that he was, indeed, Indy's assistant.

"We've managed to secure three seats," Weber continued. "But there might be a slight inconvenience, as you will be riding on a cargo full of live poultry."

"Is he kidding?" Willie asked shrilly.

Weber caught her in an icy glare. "Madame, it was the best I could do at such short notice." Suddenly his stern expression melted and he smiled eagerly. "Heavens!" he cried, "Aren't you Willie Scott, the famous American female vocalist?"

Willie bestowed one of her full wattage smiles on Weber.

They rushed toward the passenger steps of the waiting plane when the black sedan carrying Lao Che and his men pulled up to the gate. They sprang out of the sedan and hurried toward the plane.

But Indy knew they were too late. The three propeller engines were already turning. They'd be in the air in minutes.

Indy realized that he was feeling like his old self again. The antidote had worked!

He stood at the plane's doorway and shot his enemies a heroic mock salute. "Nice try, Lao Che," he called, triumphantly taunting his nemesis.

Turning, Indy pulled the door shut behind him as he entered the plane.

He did not see the pilot wave conspiratorially at Lao Che while the plane taxied down the runway. Nor did he hear Lao Che chuckle as he whispered, "Good-bye, Dr. Jones." And, most importantly, he didn't see the logo written on the plane door he had so quickly pulled shut behind him: LAO CHE AIR FREIGHT.

CHAPTER FOUR

*O*nce they were in the air, Indy opened the cockpit to greet the pilots. They were two short, chunky men who smiled warmly and assured him that everything was fine. They would reach Bangkok in several hours.

With a satisfied nod, Indy left them to fly the plane. He rubbed the back of his neck and yawned. What a crazy night. He thought about Wu Han, but there was nothing he could do to help his old friend now. When he got to Bangkok, he'd wire money to help Wu Han's family. He wished he'd gotten hold of that diamond; he'd have been able to send them a lot more if he had.

Indy stepped into the plane's restroom, peeled off his tux, and donned more familiar and comfortable attire. It felt great to pull on his canvas pants, work shirt, and leather jacket. Kicking off his fancy dress shoes, he sighed as he slipped his feet into the comfort of his well-worn leather work boots. Good old Short Round. He'd packed everything just as Indy had instructed.

Plunking his favorite fedora hat onto his head, he stepped out from the restroom with his tux draped over his arms. He made his way to the front of the plane where Short Round slept and Willie sat pouting, looking extremely unhappy.

All around them, crates of chickens clucked with agitation at being airborne. Feathers flew everywhere and the stench was overwhelming. On the ceiling overhead, nets rocked back and forth, loaded with fruits and vegetables. Burlap sacks of rice were piled three-sacks deep and five high all along the walls. The cargo hold was packed so tightly that only the narrowest of aisles remained to walk up and down.

Willie looked up and surveyed Indy's change of outfit. She raised her eyebrows skeptically as he put down his tux and hooked his coiled bullwhip over a crate. "So what are you supposed to be — a lion tamer?" she taunted him snidely, pulling his tux jacket over her shoulders for warmth.

Indy sneered back at her. She was really starting to get on his nerves. "I'm allowing you to tag along, so why don't you give your mouth a rest? Okay, doll?" he snapped at her. He'd just about had it with her wisecracks and complaints.

Willie jumped to her feet, her hands on her hips. "What do you mean, *tag along*?" she demanded indignantly. "You're the one who *dragged* me along on this insane escapade!"

He shrugged indifferently. Those were the breaks. She was probably better off getting away from Lao Che, anyway, even if she didn't realize it.

"And as for *allowing* me to tag along," she went on, a superior tone creeping into her angry voice, "ever since you got into my club you haven't been able to take your eyes off of me."

Everything she'd said was true, but Indy wasn't about to admit to it. She was beautiful. And it was true, too, that she hadn't had much choice about coming along. Still, he didn't like having it all thrown back in his face the way she doing now.

"Oh, yeah?" he said laconically, settling into a corner beside Short Round and pulling his hat down over his eyes. He'd show her just how unable to keep his eyes off her he was. In fact, his eyes were beginning to close on their own. It was a perfect time for a nap.

Indy dreamed that he was home at Marshall College, where he was a professor of archaeology. In his dream, he was doing research in the high-ceilinged library. But from somewhere in the aisles among the shelves of books, he could hear Willie Scott's voice. She was crying out, her voice becoming more agitated with every moment. "Oh, no! Oh, NOOOO!" she wailed.

And then suddenly he was shaking uncontrollably. He didn't know why. Was it an earthquake?

Indy's eyes snapped open. Willie had grabbed him by the collar and was bouncing him up and down. "Mister! Oh, Mister!" she shouted into his face.

"You call him Dr. Jones," Short Round told her sleepily, awakened by her shouting.

"Okay. Dr. Jones! Dr. Jones!" she shouted frantically. "Wake up! Please!"

Befuddled with sleep, Indy struggled to come fully awake. "Are we there already?"

"No!" Willie shouted. "No one is flying the plane!"

This unbelievable news instantly snapped Indy awake. In a second, he was on his feet. Willie pulled him to the cockpit and flung open the door.

"I went into the restroom to change into your tux pants and shirt and when I was done I thought I'd say hi to the pilots . . . but when I opened the door, there was no one to say hi to," she explained in a high-pitched wail.

Indy rushed past her into the cockpit. "Oh, boy," Indy muttered when he saw the two empty seats. Much as he'd like to deny it, this plane was too small for them to be hiding anywhere.

The pilot and co-pilot had obviously bailed out, leaving them there to crash!

"They're all gone!" Willie wailed, her voice climbing hysterically as it echoed his desperate thoughts.

There was no time to stand there gaping in dismay, so Indy jumped into the pilot's seat. Below him was a range of snow-covered mountains. He didn't know exactly where they were, but he was pretty sure this wasn't the way to Bangkok.

"You know how to fly, don't you?" Willie asked hopefully.

He surveyed the plane's many dials and switches. He'd always meant to learn to fly but somehow had never gotten around to it. There was no sense in lying to her. "No," Indy admitted. "Do you?"

She threw her hand over her mouth, gagging with fear. Willie's eyes went wide in terror. "Oh, no!" she cried, sinking into the jump seat behind him.

"How hard can it be?" Indy asked philosophically. He'd been in tighter spots than this before. At the moment he couldn't think of any, but he must have been.

"I'm going to faint!" Willie moaned.

The secret was to stay cool. Those pilots hadn't looked like geniuses. If they could navigate the dials of this flying crate, so could he. "Altimeter: okay," he checked. "Airspeed: okay. Fuel . . ."

The fuel gauge didn't appear to be working.

It read E . . . for EMPTY.

He tapped it and a red light came on.

Indiana swallowed hard. Apparently it really was empty.

At the same moment, the engine began to sputter. Looking sharply to his right, he saw one of the propellers stop turning.

Through the front windshield, he could see that they were dipping ever lower over the snow-covered mountains. The remaining two propellers conked out and the plane nosed downward even more sharply. "I think we've got a big problem," he told Willie, realizing that this was something of an understatement. "Look for parachutes, Shorty," Indy called to Short Round at the back of the plane.

The boy frantically dug through an equipment bin, but came up empty. He turned toward Indy, shaking his head.

Indy left the cockpit and came up behind Short Round to survey the bin's contents. It did indeed appear to be lacking in parachutes. Obviously the pilots had seen to that.

Pulling out a large box, Indiana read the cover and began to break the box open. "Shorty, come on. Give me a hand," he instructed. Inside was an inflatable raft. Not exactly ideal for escaping from a plane about to crash land in the snow-covered mountains, but it wasn't as though he had much else to choose from.

Working fast, they unpacked the bright yellow emergency life raft, spreading it flat on the floor of the plane. "Shorty, get our stuff," he told the boy as he slid open the cargo bay door. Instantly, a fierce wind flattened him against the side of the door.

Gripping the doorway, Indy peered out. Below, the snowy mountains loomed ever closer. It would be a matter of minutes before they crashed.

Short Round arrived with their knapsack of supplies and tossed it on top of the flat, deflated raft. Together they dragged it to the door.

Willie fought her way to them, her hands raised against the wind blasting into the cabin, her blond hair blowing wildly around her head. "A boat?!" Willie shouted when she saw what they were doing. "We're not sinking! We're crashing!"

Indy ignored her and turned to Short Round. There was no time for arguing or explaining his plan. She was a grown woman. If she didn't want to take part in his plan, he wasn't about to force her. "Grab on, Shorty! Grab on!" he instructed as he stepped into the boat. Short Round leaped in with him and grabbed Indy around the neck.

The mountainside seemed to be rushing up to meet the downward spiraling plane. Indy knew he had to wait

until just minutes before they crashed for his plan to suc-
ceed. It was time to go!

Willie screamed, jumping on just as Indy yanked the
inflation cord and propelled the raft out of the plane by
pitching his weight forward and pulling against the door's
frame.

Willie and Short Round hugged Indy from behind
while he kept a white-knuckle grip on the sides of the raft.
The wind beat at him mercilessly, but he couldn't let go —
no matter what. All their lives depended on his not losing
his grip on the raft. Indy just hoped that the rubber seams
were tough enough not to come ripping apart under the
pressure of the fierce wind and their speed. After all, it
hadn't exactly been built for this kind of punishment.

Below them, the plane crashed into a snowbank, sending up a spray of snow. They watched in horror as it
exploded in a ball of fire, with metal and other debris
shooting in a million directions.

Their raft descended more slowly through the air, buf-
feted by the roaring wind all around. Nonetheless, they
were jolted when it landed, bouncing hard against the
mountainside before rocketing down the slope at tremendous speed.

"Slow it down!" Short Round pleaded, clutching
Indy's neck so hard he was afraid he'd choke.

There was no way to slow the raft, but Indy felt it

losing velocity as they covered ground. Eventually it would slow to a stop. His mood soared as he realized that they'd made it. His crazy plan had worked and they were going to be okay!

Smiling, he glanced over his shoulder at ashen-faced Willie and grim Short Round. "That wasn't so bad, was it?" he asked jauntily.

He wasn't expecting the look of sheer terror that swept over their faces.

Turning swiftly back toward the front, he saw what they were seeing.

The yellow raft was sailing out into the open air off the end of a sheer cliff!

For a second it seemed to hang in mid air, and then it plummeted, falling downward until it landed with a huge splash in a raging torrent of white water.

The raft bounced over rocks in the river, twisting and turning helplessly through narrow gaps and sudden drops. The wild spray soaked them as they desperately clung to the raft.

Waves of white foam crashed over the side of the raft, soaking them to the bone. More than once, Indy was sure they would be thrown up against one of the many jagged rocks in their path. He had to stick his legs outside the raft to push them away from slippery boulders.

Indy was a strong swimmer, but getting out of this powerful current alive would be tough. And he didn't know if Short Round or Willie could swim at all. If he had to swim with one of them under his arm, he wasn't sure if he could make it.

"Put on the brakes!" Willie shrieked. "I hate being wet! I hate the water! And I hate you!"

"Good!" Indy shot back. "Good!" What did he care if she hated him? He had bigger problems to worry about!

CHAPTER FIVE

Finally, the raft slowed its mad, rushing ride and drifted from the main part of the river into a narrower tributary. The current flowed more gently there, swirling the raft in its languid eddy.

As the raft glided toward a clearing, Indy finally breathed a sigh of relief and relaxed against the side of the raft. On the other side of him, Willie stared out glumly, watching the river go by. Short Round sat between them creating a buffer. "All right, Shorty?" Indy asked him. "You okay?"

Short Round nodded and Indy smiled at him. What a great kid he was; brave as could be. And he never complained — unlike a certain unpleasant person sulking on the other side of the raft.

"Where are we, anyway?" Willie asked, still staring out onto the river.

The raft floated to a gentle stop in a pool of slowly

swirling water. Indy wasn't exactly sure where they were; though he wasn't about to admit that to Willie. He'd keep his eyes out for any landmarks.

They first thing he had to do was check what rations Short Round had packed. They were pretty thin — after all, he had only anticipated needing enough snacks to last them until they settled into a nice hotel in Bangkok. It didn't look like there were *any* hotels near their current location.

Short Round and Willie both gasped loudly. Indy swung around to see what had caused their alarm.

A very tall, old man stood on the nearby shore, studying them with a piercing gaze. His long, receding white hair made a halo around his dark face. He wore many strands of heavy beads over a rough, flowing robe. There was something dignified, almost mystical, in his somber demeanor.

Indy immediately knew where they were. He recognized this man as a shaman, a high priest, from the mountains of India. In a silent greeting, he placed his palms together and moved his hands up to touch his forehead.

Silently, the shaman led Willie, Short Round, and Indy down a narrow path through desolate mountainous terrain to his village. All around them, the earth was scorched; the spiky, charred remains of tree trunks were all that remained of a forest that had once stood there.

Soon they came to a village at the base of a mountain. A single road ran to it and the villagers stared with awed curiosity at the newcomers as they entered. It was a desperately poor village; the buildings were all simple mud huts. Like the path they'd just traveled, there were no trees or plants of any kind, only their burnt remains.

Indiana noticed that the villagers seemed particularly interested in Short Round, and he quickly realized that he did not see any other children around. One elderly village woman clutched Short Round affectionately to her side. Unnerved, Short Round pulled away quickly.

The shaman invited them into a thatched hut that was larger than any of the others they had seen. In the dying sunset, long shadows crossed the dim room.

Another white-haired, robed man greeted them. He seemed to be their chieftain. Sitting in half circle on a shabby rug on the floor were six other older, robed men. Indy was sure they were the ruling elders of the village. The shaman indicated that Willie, Short Round, and Indy should be seated near the elders.

The chieftain waved his hand, and three village women hurried in carrying wooden bowls filled with food, one for each of the visitors. Indy had noticed that the people were speaking Hindi and thanked them in that language.

Willie looked into her bowl, aghast at the lumpy, brown food in front of her. "I can't eat this," she hissed quietly as her face crumpled with disgust.

"That's more food than these people eat in a week," he informed her, hoping their hosts didn't speak English. "They're starving."

Willie looked around at the thin face of the woman that had given her the food and offered the bowl back to her. "I'm sorry. You can have my —"

"Eat it!" Indy interrupted her sharply.

Willie pouted at him and put down the bowl. "I'm not hungry," she stated, which they both knew was a lie.

He sympathized with her, in a way. It didn't look very appetizing. He'd taken a quick swallow and it didn't taste any better than it looked. In fact, he wasn't even sure what it was, and for him that was a new experience — normally he could identify all sorts of local cuisines. But it was all these people had and they'd offered it as a sign of friendship. The three of them were lost and stranded in these mountains and the villagers were treating them well. It was important to stay on favorable terms. "You're insulting them and you're embarrassing me," he insisted pointedly. "Eat it!"

"Eat it," Short Round echoed. Indy nodded at him approvingly. Short Round was just a kid, but he had enough sense to size up the situation and know what had to be done.

Willie picked up some of the food in her fingers, following Indy and Short Round's example. She examined it and then put it in her mouth.

Indiana continued pushing his food into his mouth and tried not to think about the taste. The sooner it was consumed, the better. If they didn't eat this food, it might be a long time before they were offered anything else and they had to save their stash of snacks for as long as possible.

He watched Willie struggle to get the food down. She grimaced and wrinkled her nose, but she was eating. He had to give her at least a little credit. She was doing what she had to do.

Wind blew through the hut as the golden glow of the sunset gave way to a growing darkness. "Bad news coming," Short Round whispered ominously, unsettled by the howls of the wind. "Bad news coming."

Indy looked to the chieftain. "Can you provide us with a guide to take us to Delhi?" he asked, switching back to Hindi. "I'm a professor. I have to get back to my university."

"Yes, Sajnu will guide you," the chieftain said helpfully.

The old shaman spoke now for the first time. His voice was raspy and low. He told them that the village was called Mayapore. "On the way to Delhi, you will stop at Pankot," he added.

"Pankot is not on the way to Delhi," Indy replied, puzzled.

"You will go to Pankot Palace," the shaman insisted.

Indy knew the old stories about Pankot Palace. He also knew those stories had ended sometime ago. "I thought the place was deserted in eighteen-fifty," he said.

"No," the shaman stated firmly. "Now there is new maharajah — and again the palace has the power of the dark light."

The old man gazed around sadly at his unfortunate people who stood at the doorway, eager to see what was happening within. "It is that place kill my people."

"What has happened here?" Indiana dared to ask.

"The evil start in Pankot," the shaman revealed. "Then, like monsoon, it moves darkness over all country."

"The evil?" Indiana asked. "What evil?"

Short Round leaned close and whispered to Indy. "Bad news," he said, nodding assuredly, grimly satisfied that his prediction was being born out by the shaman's words. "You listen to Short Round. You live longer."

Indy nodded, shushing him gently as the shaman continued his tale of woe. "They came from palace and took *sivalinga* from our village."

Willie looked to Indy. "They took what?" she asked.

"It's a stone," he explained, "a sacred stone that protects the village."

"It is why Shiva brought you here," the shaman spoke, referring to an important deity of the Hindu religion.

Indiana disagreed politely but firmly. "We weren't brought here. Our plane crashed."

"It crashed," Willie affirmed.

"No! No!" the shaman disagreed. "We prayed to Shiva to help us find the stone. It was Shiva who made you fall from the sky. So, you will go to Pankot Palace to *sivalinga* and bring back to us. You bring back to us."

Indy opened his mouth to argue. All he wanted was to travel to Delhi where they could get a good meal, sleep in a hotel-room bed, and then book a flight back to the United States. He hadn't been home in a long while and things hadn't exactly turned out as he'd hoped. The safe, steady routines of his university life seemed very attractive at the moment.

But somehow, the words wouldn't come out of his mouth. He glanced over his shoulder at the anxious faces of the villagers. These people needed help more desperately than any he had ever met.

He didn't know what to do. It might be best to decide in the morning after he'd had a chance to sleep and think about it further. He hoped that in the clear light of day, this shaman wouldn't seem so desperate. He'd become just another old man who wanted him to chase after some stone that his people had invested with a lot of silly, superstitious beliefs.

"Come. I show you place where stone was once," the shaman said, standing on his spindly, yet sturdy, legs. The chieftain and elders trailed him out of the hut. Indy, Willie, and Short Round mingled with the villagers, who also followed as the shaman led them to the very edge of their village.

Short Round tugged on Indy's jacket. "Dr. Jones, did they make the plane crash to get you here?" he asked.

"No, Shorty," Indy assured him. "It's just a ghost story. Don't worry about it."

Everyone stopped walking and circled around a crude stone shrine hacked out of a large boulder. The niche that had been carved into the rock was empty, but an indentation indicated the cone shape of the stone that had been stolen. Indy ran his palm around the inside of the place where the stone had been. "Was the stone very smooth, like a rock from a sacred river?" he asked.

"Yes," the chieftain confirmed.

"Did it have three lines across it?" Indy asked.

To this, the chieftain nodded.

"Did the three lines represent the three levels of the universe?"

Once again the chieftain nodded excitedly.

"Yes. I've seen stones like this one you lost," Indy said. "But why would a maharajah take the sacred stone from here?"

"They say we must pray to their evil god," the old shaman told him sadly. "We say we will not."

"Excuse me," Willie spoke up. "I don't understand how one rock could destroy a whole village."

The old man's eyes filled with tears that glistened against his dark eyes. He looked off into the distance and began speaking in Hindi.

As the shaman spoke, Indy translated for Willie and Short Round. "When the sacred stone was taken from the village, wells dried up and the river turned to sand," he said. "The crops were swallowed by the Earth. The animals lay down and turned to dust. Then one night there was a fire in the fields. The men went out to fight the fire. When they came back, the women were crying in the darkness."

The old shaman paused as though what he had to say next was too terrible to speak of. Indy prodded him, asking in Hindi why the woman had been crying.

Indy could hardly believe the shaman's reply. It explained why the old woman had hugged Short Round to her side so passionately. "The children," Indy told his companions. "He says they stole all their children."

That night, Indy's companions went to sleep early, completely exhausted. But his restless mind wouldn't let him relax, so he walked out into the silent, sleeping village. Under a blue-black sky studded with brilliantly bright stars, he paced.

There was so much to decide. And he felt torn in two different directions.

These people sorely needed his help. He didn't believe they had conjured him out of the sky, but he had to admit he was the perfect person for the task they required. A more well-suited recruit was unlikely to stumble upon this desolate little village. Who could be a better candidate than he — with his intimate knowledge of ancient lore and track record with valuable antiquities — to get their sacred stone back for them?

Still . . . he was tired, worn out. He'd just met these people hours ago. Why should he risk his life for them? If this maharajah had managed to wipe out an entire village of strong, able-bodied men and women and stolen their children right out from under them, what chance did he have against such a formidable foe? He was only one man — a man responsible for a rambunctious kid and a spoiled nightclub singer.

No. It was nuts. *Crazy*. He wouldn't do it.

He stopped and leaned against the wall of one of the mud buildings, thinking. This was the right decision. Besides, he had to get back to Marshall. The new semester would begin in a few weeks. He'd committed to teaching three classes and he wasn't even remotely prepared.

Indy suddenly pushed himself off the wall, alert to the sound of something moving nearby. Ordinarily, he would have dismissed it as an animal scurrying through the night, but all the animals around this village were dead.

He peered into the night and saw a dark form stumbling toward him; whatever it was moved erratically, weaving and stumbling, as though it were injured, exhausted, or both. Indy squinted, moving toward the sound. The figure emerged from the darkness and he was barely able to register that it was a young boy before he collapsed into Indy's arms.

Indy saw that the boy was half-starved: emaciated, his large, black eyes exaggerated by his bony, skeletal face. The boy reached up to Indy. His fingers were bruised and cut. He opened them and released something into Indiana's hand. "Sankara," he whispered through parched lips, his voice a rasp. "Sankara."

From out of the darkness, a woman gasped and rushed to the boy. From the way the boy stretched his arms to her, Indy was certain this was his mother. He would have been touched by their emotional reunion as the joyfully sobbing woman cradled her son, but he was too distracted by the artifact the boy had just given him. It was a palm-sized piece of tattered cloth; an old fragment of a miniature painting.

Indy recognized it immediately — and it made him deeply uneasy. "Sankara," he whispered.

Awakened by the emotional cries of the village woman, people were emerging from their huts. Indy wanted to get away to examine this cloth more closely.

He climbed atop a hill just outside the village until he reached the scorched remains of a tree. Looking down at the village, he saw that all the huts were now illuminated and buzzing with activity. He couldn't get the poor kid's desperate face out of his mind.

If he'd escaped from Pankot Palace, he'd traveled a long way on his own, and probably gone without food or water for days.

Rimmed by moonlight, Short Round appeared, climbing up the hillside toward him. "The boy escaped from the evil place," he said, breathlessly confirming Indiana's suspicions. "Many other children still there. What we do, Dr. Jones?"

Indy's mouth went dry. He had no idea what to tell Short Round.

"What you think?" Short Round pressed him impatiently.

"I think that somebody believes the good-luck rock from this village is one of the lost Sankara Stones."

"What is Sankara?"

Indy wondered how he could best explain the power that the Sankara Stones allegedly possessed. It was beyond words. But Short Round was clearly waiting for an answer.

"It's fortune and glory, kid," Indiana said at last. "Fortune and glory."

CHAPTER SIX

*I*n the morning, the villagers provided two huge, Asian elephants with massive curved tusks for Indiana and Willie to travel on, and one baby elephant for Short Round. With a helpful boost-up from two village men, Indy easily saddled his animal, while Short Round mounted his much smaller version. Willie's ascent, however, wasn't so graceful. She slid, arms and legs unable to find a hold, sputtering and complaining all the while, as villagers labored in vain to help her up.

"Willie, quit monkeyin' around on that thing," Indy mockingly scolded, trying to suppress a grin. Begrudgingly, he had to admit — if only to himself — that she had a game spirit even though she did love to complain.

With a desperate squeal of effort, Willie hoisted herself onto the elephant's back, but pulled too hard with her right hand, causing her to spin around so that her head faced the animal's rear end!

Good enough, Indy decided, eager to get going. She was up on the elephant. It didn't really matter which direction she faced; a village guide named Sajnu walked beside her and would guide her elephant wherever it needed to go.

Indiana gave the lead guide the signal to move out. Together, the elephants, along with five other village guides on foot, began their journey.

"Oh, wait a second, Indy," Willie wailed pitifully, struggling to hold on while traveling backward. "I can't go to Delhi like this!"

"We're not going to Delhi," he informed her. "We're going to Pankot Palace."

He'd made his decision at dawn. He couldn't get the escaped boy's starved, desperate eyes out of his mind; there was no way he could refuse these people who needed his help so much. It just wouldn't be right.

"Pankot?" Willie shrieked. "I can't go to Pankot. I'm a singer. I need to call my agent! Is there a phone? Anybody? I need a phone."

Indy heard her hollering, but like the distant buzz of a mosquito, he paid no attention to it. Instead, he was looking down at the villagers who had come to see them off. He waved as he took in their hopeful expressions. They were all counting on him. He just hoped he would prove worthy of their trust.

As the sun rose, the day grew increasingly warm and

steamy. Indy was on the lead elephant but Willie soon passed him, led by Sajnu. She had somehow turned herself forward, but still looked mightily distressed.

Indy had to smile as he watched her sniff her armpits, and then realize it was the elephant whose strong smell was disturbing her. His smile widened even more when he saw her sprinkling perfume from her back pocket all over the odorous animal — as though that would make the slightest difference. And his smile turned into a burst of laughter when the elephant's trunk swung back over its head, sniffed the flowery fragrance, and trumpeted its disgust into the air. "Oh, quit complaining," Willie yelled at the creature. "This is expensive stuff!"

Short Round and his small elephant drew up alongside Indy and, unlike Willie, he seemed to have befriended the creature. "You come to America with me and we get a job in circus," he spoke to it soothingly and Indy couldn't help but grin. "You like that? You like America? You're my best friend."

But Indy was distracted from watching Short Round by a whirring, flapping sound overhead. Gazing up, he saw a flock of large creatures whose wide, black wings obscured the blue sky.

"Oooh! What big birds!" Willie remarked excitedly.

"Those aren't birds, sweetheart. Those are giant vampire bats," Indy told her.

Willie shuddered and went pale, ducking her head.

Hah! Got ya! Indy thought, gloating triumphantly. Vampire bats were small. These large bats were flying foxes — all they liked to bite was fruit. But Willie didn't know that. He'd gotten her back for throwing his gun out the window, or maybe for all the complaining she'd done, or maybe just for saying she hated him. Now they were even, he figured.

They traversed the dense, moist jungle, moving steadily westward, until an immense red sun hung low in the sky. Indiana was beginning to feel the strain of bouncing along, rigidly upright, for so many hours. Surely the guides on foot had to be getting fatigued. Checking over his shoulder, he glanced back to see how Willie was faring.

Her blond curls were disheveled and damp with sweat. She slumped forward wearily, sprinkling the last of her perfume over her elephant's neck. The elephant snorted, protesting the strange floral smell raining down on it. "Oh, pipe down, you big baboon," she scolded the elephant. "This doesn't hurt. You know what you really need? You really need a bath."

As though it understood her words, the elephant dipped its trunk into a shallow, muddy, river running alongside the dirt path on which they traveled. After drinking deeply, it swung its trunk over its head and unleashed a torrential spray of water right on top of her.

Screaming, she slid off the elephant's side, splashing right into the river.

Short Round convulsed with laughter at the sight of Willie, sputtering and flailing in the river. "Very funny!" he cried, rocking gleefully. "Very funny! Very funny! All wet!"

Willie pulled herself into a sitting position there in the river. She didn't even try to get up. "I was happy in Shanghai," she wailed, on the edge of tears. "I had a little house and garden. All my friends were rich." She shook her head mournfully and Indy could tell this had been the last straw. "We went to parties all the time." She slapped the water and started sobbing, speaking in gulps through her tears. "I hate being outside. I'm a singer. I could lose my voice."

If only that would happen, Indy thought hopefully. Still, she looked so pitiful there, sobbing in the water, that he had to feel sorry for her. "I think we'll camp here for the night," he told the guides.

Indy slid off his elephant and went to help Willie out of the water. She got up on her own power and splashed past him, stomping onto the embankment, spraying him with water as she went. *Suit yourself*, he thought.

Indy made a fire for them in a circle of thick, vine-strewn jungle trees. The guides gave them more of the strange, brown mush they had eaten the evening before and then retreated to bed down for the night a short way off.

After eating and tending to the elephants, Willie went off to find a stream in which to wash up. Indiana and Short Round settled down to play a heated game of poker, betting with the coins in their pockets. By the time Willie returned, Indy's dripping tuxedo slung over one arm and wrapped in a blanket, they were into their third round.

"Whadda you got?" Short Round challenged Indy, holding his cards close.

"Two sixes," Indy said, showing his cards.

Short Round laughed victoriously. "Ah, ha! Three aces! I win!" He clapped his hands, his face lit with good-natured greed. "In two more games, I have *all* your money!"

Willie settled down to watch them play. She sat in front of her elephant, which stood beside a tree at the out-skirts of the clearing. As she attempted to concentrate on the game, the pachyderm nuzzled her playfully with its trunk. "Cut it out!" she scolded, impatiently pushing its trunk away. After it had so rudely dumped her in the muddy river, she wanted nothing to do with it.

Indy wasn't paying attention to Willie. His mind was focused on the game. Short Round was beating the pants off him; it was true. His pride was injured and he felt determined not to be trounced by a child, even one as wily as Short Round. "It's poker, Shorty. Anything can happen," he said, feigning confidence. Short Round was good at this!

Willie stepped between them and began hanging Indiana's drenched tux shirt and pants on a tree branch. "So, where did you find your, ah, little bodyguard?" she asked with a nod toward Short Round.

"I didn't find him. I caught him," Indy answered in a matter-of-fact tone as he dealt cards.

"What?" Willie asked, perplexed by this reply.

"Shorty's family were killed when the Japanese bombed Shanghai. He's been living on the street ever since then, since he was four. I caught him trying to pick my pocket. Didn't I, Short Stuff?"

Indy remembered how stealthily Short Round had slipped his little hand right into his bomber jacket. He'd thought Indy was just another clueless tourist — an easy target. When he realized his mistake, Short Round tried to get away, and Indy had never seen anyone run so fast or amble over crates and carts with such dexterity. But Indy's bullwhip was faster, and Short Round was caught before long. It was obvious, though, that the kid was just trying to survive. And Indy had to admire his nerve. He knew he would make a perfect assistant.

While recalling his first encounter with Short Round, Indy languidly watched Willie hang clothes. She stooped to pick up the tux pants from a pile and came up holding one of the large fruit bats they'd seen earlier, holding each one of its velvety wings. At first she didn't realize what she held, absently spreading its wings wide, assuming they were the two legs of the pants.

In a second, though, she turned ashen as she beheld the creature in her hands. It hissed at her and began flapping its wings in an attempt to free itself. Screaming frantically, she tossed the bat aside and began to race around the campsite as the bat flew off into the night.

Short Round and Indy both suppressed grins while Willie continued to shriek at the top of her voice and run around flapping her arms hysterically. "The biggest trouble with her is the noise," Indy commented wryly to Short Round.

Willie shrieked again when she came face-to-face with a small monkey on a low lying branch. Whirling away from it, she ran right into a large lizard resting tranquilly on the trunk of a tree. Indy wouldn't have thought it possible for her shrieks to become any louder or more shrill than the ones he'd already heard, but when she saw the lizard, his eardrums actually *hurt*.

He tried to block out her piercing yells by focusing on the card game. But in the next moment, Short Round began shouting, too. "Hey, you cheat, Dr. Jones!" he accused, pointing at Indy's cards.

Indy checked his cards and saw that he did, indeed have four instead of three. "Oh, they stuck together," he realized.

Short Round didn't believe it. "You pay now!" he demanded. "No stuck!"

"A mistake," Indy insisted.

All the while their voices were growing louder as they shouted over Willie's screams. "I very little," Short Round yelled. "You cheat very big." He was turning red with anger. Normally, Indy respected Short Round's relentless ferocity, but at the moment it was getting on his nerves.

"Dr. Jones, you cheat! You pay money! You owe me ten cents!" Short Round continued on.

As Short Round flailed his arms in anger, Indy saw a flash of white. Deftly grabbing Short Round's wrist, he extricated a fourth card from his long white cotton shirt sleeve. "Look at this!" Indy shouted indignantly. "Look at this! You accuse *me* of cheating!"

Never one to back down, even in the face of incriminating evidence against him, Short Round continued his furious tirade in Chinese. Indy automatically made the language shift with him, shouting back in Chinese.

As the heated disagreement between Indy and Short Round escalated, so did Willie's howls of horrified terror. A startled owl, upset by the commotion, fluttered its wings in her face. Terrified, Willie stumbled backwards only to trip over the lizard who had moved down from the tree.

"You make me poor. No fun," Short Round shouted in Chinese.

He was right, Indy decided. All this fighting was definitely not fun. "I quit," he announced, throwing down his cards.

Announcing that he also quit, Short Round stomped away from the campfire and crawled into his blanket roll. Seconds later, Willie slid hers onto the dirt beside Indy, panting breathlessly. "This place is completely surrounded," she declared miserably. "The entire place is crawling with living creatures."

A slight smile played on Indiana's lips. "That's why they call it the jungle, sweetheart," he remarked.

Off in the distance, some creature snarled fiercely. "Oh my God! What else is out there?" Willie wailed.

He reached out to pat her back, attempting to calm her, but his touch only startled her once again. She leaped up with a shout and bounded to the other side of the campfire where she stood breathing heavily with fear.

He really did want to do something to help her calm down. She was getting so worked up! If she didn't relax, she'd be headed for a nervous collapse before dawn. Some friendly chit-chat might do the trick. "Willie. What is that?" he asked. "Is that short for something?"

"Willie is my professional name...*Indiana*," she revealed a bit defensively, pointing out his own unusual name in a derisive tone, as if to say: *You of all people should not be commenting about strange names.*

Groggily, Short Round popped up from his roll of blankets. "Hey, lady, you call him Dr. Jones," he insisted loyally, their recent fight apparently forgotten.

"*My* professional name," Indy told her as he flipped a ten-cent coin to Short Round in appreciation.

Willie once again settled down, cross-legged, in front of her elephant. It instantly resumed its attempt to get her to play with it by tapping her on the head and curling its trunk around her neck. Absently, as though shooing off a persistently buzzing fly, she swatted the annoying trunk away as she spoke. "Why are you dragging us off to this deserted palace?" she asked. "Is it for fortune and glory?"

"Fortune and glory," Short Round echoed sleepily, about to drift off to sleep.

From his inside jacket pocket, Indiana carefully withdrew the scrap of cloth the escaped village boy had given to him. He pointed out the drawing of ancient figures done in red, blue, and gold with hieroglyphic writing beneath it, handing it to her. "This is a piece of old manuscript," he explained. "The pictograph there represents Sankara, an ancient priest."

She gazed down curiously at the frayed material with

its drawings of figures from long ago. As she tried to concentrate on the scene depicted on the cloth, her elephant
ran its trunk around her neck again. "Scram," she told it,
pushing it away while she studied the picture before her.

"Gently. Gently," Indy cautioned. "That material is
hundreds of years old."

"Is that some kind of writing?" she asked, pointing to
the hieroglyphs.

"Yeah, Sanskrit," he replied.

Willie nodded while slapping the elephant away. "Cut
it out!" she muttered with growing irritation.

"It's part of the legend of Sankara. He climbs Mount
Kalisa where he meets Shiva, the Hindu god," Indy
continued.

Willie located Shiva in the drawing. "What's he handing the priest?" she asked.

"Rocks. Shiva told him to go forth and combat evil.
And to help Kalisa, he gave him the five sacred stones with
magical properties."

A quizzical expression came over Willie's face. "Magic
rocks?" she questioned skeptically.

Indy nodded. The ancient texts might have described
it more fancifully, and academic terminology more for-
mally. But that's what it actually boiled down to: magic
rocks.

Willie's voice took on an unexpected softness as she

recalled a memory from her childhood. "My grandpa was a magician. He spent his entire life with a rabbit in his pocket and pigeons up his sleeve. He made a lot of people happy and died a poor man. Magic rocks. Fortune and glory."

Willie turned away, her face full of bitter disgust. Indiana could see she believed it was all superstitious non-sense leading to disappointment. But he'd seen enough in his many adventures around the globe to know that even the most outlandish tales often had a hint of truth — or at least an incredible archaeological find — behind them. It was the reason he'd made archaeology his life's work.

He'd read the tale of Sankara in the original Sanskrit years ago. He'd read accounts dating back hundreds of years by people who swore they had witnessed for themselves the staggering magical power of the magic stones.

Willie pulled her bedroll off further from the campfire. "Sweet dreams, Dr. Jones," she said with a yawn.

"Where are you going?" he asked.

She tugged her beddings even further away.

"I'd sleep closer if I were you," he advised, "for safety's sake."

She chuckled knowingly. "Dr. Jones, I'd be safer sleep-ing with a snake," she replied.

As she spoke, Indy leaped to his feet.

His heart raced.

The thing he feared most on the planet — the one creature that truly made his knees buckle in terror and his skin grow clammy — maybe the *only* thing that could reduce him to a sniveling mass of panic, had slithered from the tree behind Willie and was making its way around her neck.

It was a snake.

And it was gliding along Willie's shoulders.

Indiana Jones detested snakes, feared and loathed them. He fought back all the gut-wrenching memories of his encounters with the slithery demons. None of them had cured him of this phobia; they'd only made it worse.

With a trembling hand, he pointed to the creature making its way down the front of Willie's chest. He tried to warn her, but the words turned to dust on his fear-parched tongue.

She looked at him questioningly. Then she felt the snake.

Indy braced for her ear-splitting scream of terror.

But Willie mistook the snake for the trunk of the pesky elephant that been tormenting her all night. Finally fed up, she gripped it with both hands and hurled it away from her, shouting, "I said cut it *out!*"

The boa flipped end over end into a clump of nearby bushes and slithered away.

Not even realizing what she'd done, Willie shook her head woefully. "I hate that elephant!"

Indy slumped back against a boulder in relief, his frenetic heartbeat gradually slowing. He wiped sweat from his brow.

He watched Willie crawl under her blankets, oblivious to the danger she had just encountered. Indy was slowly revising his opinion of her. She might be skittish over nighttime creatures, but he had a feeling that when it mattered, she could be counted on.

He couldn't be sure. Still, his gut feelings had a habit of being right.

CHAPTER SEVEN

*A*t dawn, they set off on their way once again. Tall, vine-covered trees swayed in the humid breeze as the elephants plowed through the dense, tropical forest. The squawks, growls, and chirps of teeming jungle life surrounded them.

After many hours of difficult travel, they came to a place where the thick jungle canopy broke, giving a glimpse of the sky. Indy gazed up and saw that the sun was still high. It was a good thing, too, because he estimated that they still had many miles to go. If what he surmised was correct, Pankot Palace was at the other end of the jungle, high in the mountains.

After another hour, they left the jungle and traversed a swampy valley. Several times, the elephants nearly became stuck in the muddy ground, trumpeting their displeasure as they struggled to extricate their thick, round legs from the muck. By the time they made it through the valley, all of the elephants were caked in mud.

Finally though, as a dusky glow suffused the sky, they began to ascend a mountain where the shrubbery was low and scruffy. The size and shape of the plant life told Indiana that they were very high up and climbing higher every minute. He tried breathing deeply, finding it was more difficult than he expected. The air was thinner at this altitude.

"Look!" Short Round cried out when they turned a bend in the path.

"I see it, Shorty," Indy replied. They were gazing at a resplendent cluster of high, dome-topped towers rising in the distance.

It seemed almost unreal sitting there so regally atop the mountain, especially after they had traveled so many hours without seeing so much as a single fabricated hut. The mogul-style palace was as large as a small city. The setting sun bounced off the inlaid gold of its many rounded rooftops, making it appear to radiate with unearthly light.

Turning, Indy looked to see how Willie was reacting to this majestic sight. She sat astride her elephant with her mouth agape, staring in awe. He understood her amazement. It was like something out of *Arabian Nights*, an enchanted place that had somehow survived from a time long ago.

As they climbed the steep path to the palace they stopped at what appeared, at first, to be some sort of roadside shrine. Indy did not want to pause for even a short break. At this point, he was eager to reach their destination before dark. But looking closer, Indy grew worried about the sight before him, an ominous statue throwing a wavering form in the shadowy dusk. He had seen this deity, a goddess of destruction and death, in ancient books and scrolls.

If he was seeing the deity he suspected, it was not a good sign. No, not good at all.

He motioned for the guides to stop. They barked commands to the elephants, which obediently halted. Indiana slid down the side of his elephant and walked toward the shrine to get a better look at the life-sized stone statue at the end of a narrow pathway.

As he had suspected, the many-armed, female deity before him was the Hindu goddess Kali. Kali the Destroyer had her positive aspects, destroying the bad as well as the good. This was a particularly sinister depiction of the goddess, suggesting, bloodthirsty, malevolent destruction.

A small and dangerous sect known as the Thuggee had worshipped Kali as representing all the dark powers of magic. Her presence was ominous and a very bad sign.

Indy was so engrossed in reappraising their situation that it took him a moment to realize what was hanging from her many arms. When he finally focused more closely, he staggered backward in horror.

Heads!

In each of her eight hands she gripped rotted human heads.

Fighting the wave of nausea that threatened to overwhelm him, he stepped closer and realized that someone had draped a garland around the statue's neck. He let out a quick revolted grunt when he saw what hung from her vine necklace: dead rodents, birds, and reptiles.

On top of that hideous adornment lay another string of blood-stained body parts — *animal or human?*

Who had concocted this gruesome warning? Who had killed these people and why?

"Dr. Jones, what you look at?" Short Round shouted up to him, getting off his small elephant and standing beside Willie, who had also dismounted.

"Don't come up here," he warned him firmly. This was something Indy would not soon forget and he didn't want the horrifying image emblazoned in Shorty's young mind.

He was about to inspect some ancient writing on the statue's base when a yelp from Willie made him whirl back around.

"No! No!" she cried, running after the guides who were

riding off on the backs of the elephants. They quickly out-distanced her, leaving her fuming on the path. "Indy! They're stealing our rides!" she shouted.

He shook his head and grinned at her misunderstanding. "The elephants can't go any further," he explained. "We have to walk from here."

He guessed that after seeing the gruesome warning, the guides had decided that this was as close as they wanted to get to Pankot Palace. He could hardly blame them.

Were Indiana, Willie, and Short Round fools to keep going? *Probably*, Indy thought as he motioned for Short Round and Willie to follow him up the mountain toward the palace.

CHAPTER EIGHT

It was midafternoon by the time the trio entered the silent, foreboding outer courtyard of Pankot Palace. Two guards dressed in long white robes and crimson turbans were stationed at opposite sides of the open space with broadswords strapped to their hips. If not for their presence, Indy would have thought the place was deserted.

"Hello," Indy greeted the guards. But they did not answer or acknowledge him in any way, as though he hadn't spoken at all.

Before he could make a second attempt at communicating with the guards, a very official-looking man in a dark suit stepped out of a doorway. He was small with a pinched, officious manor. He surveyed them with an amused smirk, yet when he spoke, his tone was polite, even helpful. "I should say you look rather lost. But then I cannot imagine where in the world the three of you would look at home."

Indiana suddenly realized how the three of them must appear: a blond with a mop of messy curls dressed in a man's tuxedo, a small Asian boy in a New York Yankees baseball cap, and a grown man in a fedora, bomber jacket, and boots, carrying a bullwhip.

They were a motley bunch, to be sure!

"We're not lost," Indy explained to the man. "We're on our way to Delhi. This is Miss Scott. This is Mr. . . . Round."

"Short Round," the boy concurred, with a dignified air of importance.

"My name is Indiana Jones," Indy added.

The man's eyebrows lifted in delighted surprise. "Dr. Jones — the eminent archaeologist?" he asked, clearly very aware of and impressed by Indy's reputation.

"Hard to believe, isn't it?" Willie quipped derisively.

Indy shot her an annoyed look, but said nothing. Her mouth was likely to get them into trouble around here.

The man took no notice of Willie's remark and kept his attention on Indy. "Ah, I remember first hearing your name when I was up at Oxford," he recalled excitedly. "I am Chattar Lal, Prime Minister to His Highness the Maharajah of Pankot."

"Oh," Indy said, not knowing how to respond to this news. Until he'd crash-landed into the mountain village, he hadn't known there even *was* a Maharajah of Pankot, let alone that he had a prime minister named Chattar Lal. As far as most outsiders knew, Pankot Palace and its kingdom had been abandoned a long time ago. Obviously the old shaman had known what he was talking about.

Chattar Lal extended his hand and Indy politely shook it. Then the prime minister turned to Willie, finally looking at her, and bowed, taking her hand gallantly. "I'm enchanted," he said, suavely kissing her hand.

"Thank you very much," Willie said smoothly, charmed by his elegant manners. "Thank you very much."

Indy scowled. There was something about Chattar Lal's syrupy, cheesy, overblown manners that he just didn't trust.

Chattar Lal motioned for them to follow him into the palace. Short Round began to go, but Indy held him back and politely gestured for Willie to proceed first. He'd shown her that he could be as well-mannered as that buffoon of a prime minister, Chattar Lal.

Willie graced Indy with an appreciative nod and quick smile before following the prime minister inside. "Enchanted, huh?" Indy grumbled as he and Short Round went in behind her.

The palace might have been the most splendid place Indy had ever seen firsthand. The golden ceilings were immensely high, vaulted and supported by thick, ornate columns. Every turn revealed an obviously priceless work of art: paintings and statues of every description. The floors were inlaid with gold and studded with rubies, emeralds, and pearls that made them sparkle wherever sunlight filtered through the lavish and complex cutouts of the shuttered windows.

Chattar Lal brought them up a winding spiral of stairs laid with mosaics and showed them to two separate rooms on the same tranquil corridor. Willie's lavish room was directly across from an even larger one that Indy and Short Round would share.

The prime minister told them to refresh themselves and then invited them to be his guests at a dinner party to be held in the maharajah's pavilion that evening. If they were lucky, he said, the maharajah himself might join them.

When Willie protested that she had nothing to wear to a party — she explained to Chattar Lal that her designer gown from Paris had been lost in a horrific plane crash — Chattar Lal said not to worry. He would instruct servants to bring her fresh clothing for the event.

Willie smiled at Chattar Lal so charmingly that Indy furrowed his brow at her as she exited into her room. Not once since they had met had Willie smiled at him like that. Up until now he hadn't even known she *could* smile like that. He'd thought all she could do was to complain and scream.

Then again, Indy hadn't even been able to offer her a bath, much less a new gown.

Entering the room he would share with Short Round, Indy stretched out on the luxurious, canopied bed and sighed. He hadn't been in a bed this comfortable since . . . since . . . well, maybe never. It was certainly a drastic change from the hard ground on which he'd slept for the last two nights.

He thought of the smooth, well-dressed Chattar Lal and the way Willie had smiled at him . . . not that he cared, of course. She could smile at anyone she liked. It wasn't as though she had any taste in men. Her last boyfriend had been Lao Che, for crying out loud!

Still, it bugged Indy that she treated him with such contempt while she mooned over these lowlifes. If the village shaman was right, the people so eager to charm them now were responsible for kidnapping hundreds of children—maybe more. Had she forgotten that?

Indy hadn't seen any signs of the missing children yet, but that didn't mean the palace wasn't hiding any secrets. Hopefully, dinner would be illuminating. He had some ideas about how to turn the evening's situation to his advantage. But in order to get anything out of these royal criminals, Indy would have to look the part of the esteemed professor: the eminent Dr. Jones.

He rolled over onto his side. "Shorty," he called into the alcove where Short Round was bouncing on the chaise lounge where he would sleep. "Where are my clothes?"

CHAPTER NINE

When it was time for the dinner party, a servant came to each room and rang a tinkling bell outside the door. Indy examined himself in the long mirror by his bed. He had showered, combed his hair, and donned a fresh sports jacket, creased pants, a shirt, socks, shoes, and a bow tie. He'd even dug his glasses out of the satchel Short Round had packed. Indy really only needed them for when he did a lot of reading, but they gave him a distinguished air.

He told Short Round to finish up. The boy was in the bathroom, luxuriating in a large bathtub inlaid with gold. The tub was so big that he was actually underwater, swimming in a circle. Coming up for air, he assured him that he would hurry, though Indy thought it would probably take a lot to get him out of the tub.

In the hallway, Indy knocked on Willie's door. She didn't answer so he tried again. Where could she be? Was she also submerged in a golden bathtub? Maybe she was napping.

Giving up, he went down the spiral staircase to the Pleasure Pavilion. Guards in turbans stood in front of two tall, silver doors. A third guard opened the door as he neared it.

Indiana was not the first guest to arrive. Fourteen other men were already standing in front of a dais watching swirling female dancers in colorful, diaphanous saris dance to music played by musicians dressed in traditional robes. The dancers moved together to the music, their dresses creating a fluid rainbow around their lithe, graceful bodies.

The majority of the guests also wore the traditional robes and turbans of the region, although much more elegant versions than the robes of the musicians. Chattar Lal wore no turban, but he had donned a high-collared garment. Indy identified it as a *sherwani*, a traditional style for northern Indian men. The only other guest who was not dressed in the traditional local style was an older, balding man in a uniform of a British cavalry captain.

At first, Indy went unnoticed. When he arrived, all the guests were engrossed in watching the entertainment. That was fine with him. He wanted a moment to take in his surroundings.

This room was even more spectacular than any other room of the palace Indy had seen thus far. The curtain over the dais shimmered, the golden threads softly reflecting the light from the lamps. Golden chairs lined the room, and the rug below his feet appeared to have been woven entirely from golden yarn.

When the musicians stopped playing and the audience applauded, Chattar Lal leaned close to speak to Indy. "We are fortunate tonight to have so many unexpected visitors," he said. Beside him stood a tall, middle-aged man with blazing blue eyes and thick muttonchop whiskers. He was the British cavalry captain that Indy had spotted earlier. "This is Captain Blumburtt," Chattar Lal introduced him.

The captain smiled cordially. "Eleventh Puma Rifles," he said proudly, elaborating on his specific station. "And you, sir, are Dr. Jones, I presume."

"I am, captain," Indy confirmed.

"Captain Blumburtt and his troops are on a routine inspection tour," Chattar Lal explained. "The British find it amusing to inspect us at their convenience."

Chattar Lal's smoothly pleasant tone belied the sourness of his jab, but the complaint was not lost on the captain and he reddened. "I do hope, sir, that it is not, ah, inconvenient to you, ah, sir," he sputtered in a thick English accent.

The prime minister's voice remained silkily snide. "The British worry so about their empire. It makes us all feel like well-cared-for children," he replied.

As the dancers were exiting, Short Round appeared and was nearly run over by the rush of women. He shouted at them indignantly in Chinese, but was ignored.

Willie came in right behind Short Round. Indy drew in a sharp breath when he saw her. She was stunning in a gossamer gown that appeared to have been made for an Indian princess. The lavish Mogul-style jewelry she'd been loaned sparkled on her neck and arms. She was completely refreshed and unbelievably radiant.

"You look beautiful," Indy said when she joined him.

Willie gazed around, her eyes wide as she drank in the luxurious splendor of her surroundings. "I think the maharajah's swimming in loot," she noted in a conspiratorial undertone. "Maybe it wasn't such a bad idea coming here, after all."

Indy was too mesmerized by his surroundings to pay attention to her tactless words. "You look like a princess," he told her.

"Mr. Lal," Willie said, turning toward him, "what do they call the maharajah's wife?"

"His Highness has not yet taken a wife," Chattar Lal informed her.

Willie's eyes lit with excitement and Indy was roused from his stupor. He saw at once what was in her conniving mind. The little opportunist had forgotten all about charming Chattar Lal; she'd set her sights higher. Now she was bent on dazzling the maharajah — and she hadn't even met the guy yet! Indy could practically see the wheels turning in her scheming head.

"How interesting," Willie commented, delighted at the news that the maharajah was still a single man eligible to make her his queen or maharani or whatever the term turned out to be. It wouldn't matter to Willie, Indy was sure, just as long as she got the gold and jewels.

"Well, ah, maybe the maharajah hasn't met the right woman yet," she went on, a crafty smile coming to her lips.

Indiana shook his head woefully, amazed at the obvious thought behind her remark.

A gong was sounded and the assembled guests moved into an adjoining room toward a long, low table surrounded by colorful pillows. Like everything else in the palace, the table was a study in luxury, with golden candlesticks, vases overflowing with flowers, and silverware that shone as though it were studded with diamonds.

Short Round was shown to a spot next to Willie at the far end of the table, and Indy was guided to a place near the head of the table, next to Captain Blumburtt and across from Chattar Lal. No one sat, and so Indy, Willie, and Short Round stood at their places, as well.

Everyone quieted as Chattar Lal cleared his throat, preparing to make an announcement. With an arm raised toward two solid silver doors, he intoned: "His Supreme Highness, guardian of Pankot tradition — the Maharajah of Pankot, Zalim Singh."

The doors opened as if blown by a magic wind and through them walked a figure outfitted in a spectacular, red-and-gold-brocaded, high-collared coat that came to below the knees of his legging-swaddled legs. The coat was festooned with enormous jewels, as was the ornate, shimmering turban on his head. But the most unexpected thing about the maharajah was his age; he could not have been more than thirteen!

All the guests bowed and Indy did the same.

The maharajah was a kid!

He snickered softly, amused. How was Willie reacting to this new development? He bit down on his smile as he imagined the look of disappointment and distress that must be playing across her face.

The little maharajah gazed imperiously at his bowing guests before seating himself on an array of golden pillows at the head of the table. He nodded and everyone else was free to sit. Another nod to the serving staff initiated the flow of food carried out on golden trays.

Glancing down to the end of the table where Willie and Short Round sat, he saw the servants set down a huge platter in front of them. Willie's eyes widened with panicked alarm when she saw what was on it: an enormous, steaming boa constrictor!

Did it have to be a *snake*? Indy gripped the table tight in an effort to control his terror and not make a spectacle of himself. He was glad the table was so long and hoped there would not be a similar delicacy coming his way.

Although Willie and Short Round were recoiling in horror at the dish, a fat, turbaned merchant beside Willie rubbed his hands in greedy delight as he inhaled the steam emanating from the platter. "Ah, snake surprise," he said with rapturous delight.

"What's the surprise?" Willie asked cautiously.

Indy clenched his stomach muscles to keep the insides of his belly from lurching forward when he saw a waiter slit the snake's skin and the so-called surprise erupted from inside the boa. Eels slithered out of it, flopping all along the table.

The guests stabbed them with their forks, dropping them whole into their mouths, obviously relishing the tasty treat. Indy was extremely grateful that Captain Blumburtt also displayed nothing but disgust for the creatures, swatting them off the table each time one crawled too close.

Captain Blumburtt began telling Indy some facts about the history of the palace and he was thankful for the distraction. Indy already knew most of the information, but listened intently anyway, alert for anything new he might learn that would help him understand what was going on here.

He noticed Chattar Lal listening to their conversation and looked to him politely. "Captain Blumburtt was just telling me about the importance the palace played in the mutiny," he informed him. In 1857, a revolt against the British rule of India had had its origin at Pankot Palace, though it had been suppressed by British troops.

Chattar Lal sniffed haughtily. "It seems the British never forget the Mutiny of 1857," he commented dryly, a sarcastic sneer in his voice. It was obviously a point in the palace's history that Chattar Lal was not keen to be reminded of.

Indiana figured he would learn more if Chattar Lal was in a better mood, so he turned the topic away from the mutiny. Besides, he was working on a theory, one he was eager to explore now. "I think there are other events before the mutiny, going back a century to the time of Clive, that are more interesting," he said diplomatically in his most academic, professorial tone.

It had done the trick. Chattar Lal relaxed and even

managed a tight smile. "And what events are those, Dr. Jones?" he inquired, leaning forward with interest.

Indy paused, wanting to frame his next comment just right. He had been thinking about the horrible, head-wielding statue of Kali. Its presence so near the palace surely had to mean that the ancient Thuggee cult was once again active in the area.

"If memory serves me correctly," he began in an off-handed manner, trying to sound as though his interest was purely academic, "this province was the center of activity for the Thuggee."

The Thuggee cult had been active from the 13th century all the way to the 1800's, though they had been strongest in the 1600's. Thuggee groups traveled in gangs of between ten to two hundred members. They would join wealthy travelers along the road, at first seeming helpful and friendly, and when the moment seemed right, would strangle the travelers with a yellow cloth, a symbol of their goddess, stealing the travelers' possessions. They would also assassinate anyone for money. They claimed to do all this in the service of Kali, and put aside a portion of what they stole and earned through killings in honor of their dreadful goddess.

The British encountered them when they took over India and it was the Thuggee who brought the word *thug* into the English language. In the 1830's the British began to crack down on the cult and by the 1890's these notorious killers and thieves had been mostly stamped out — but perhaps not as completely as was thought.

Chattar Lal clearly knew all about them and grew angry at the mere mention of the word "Thuggee." "Dr. Jones, you know perfectly well that the Thuggee cult has been dead for nearly a century," he snapped peevishly.

"Yes, of course," Captain Blumburtt joined the exchange. "The Thuggee was an obscenity that worshipped a Kali-like goddess with human sacrifices. The British Army nicely did away with them."

"Well, I suppose stories of the Thuggee die hard," Indiana conceded philosophically, trying to smooth things.

"There are no stories anymore," Chattar Lal insisted stiffly, offended.

"I'm not so sure," Indy disagreed. If he'd had no ulterior motive, Indy might have let the subject drop. But he needed to probe further. No matter what this phony prime minister said, he was *sure* the Thuggee had resurfaced; everything pointed to it.

It was time to stop beating around the bush. He couldn't worry about offending Chattar Lal any more. "We came from a small village," he began. "The peasants there told us Pankot Palace was growing powerful again because of an ancient evil."

A DOUBLE CROSS!

A CRASH LANDING!

AND A JUNGLE JOURNEY!

WITH SHADOWY FOES!

EVIL DEEDS!

UNLIKELY ALLIES!

AND A NARROW ESCAPE!

IF ADVENTURE HAS A NAME, IT MUST BE INDIANA JONES!

CHAPTER TEN

*T*here! It was out on the table. Indy sat back in his chair awaiting the reaction.

"Village stories, Dr. Jones," Chattar Lal insisted. "They're just . . . fear and folklore. You're beginning to worry Captain Blumburtt."

"Not worried, Mr. Prime Minister," Captain Blumburtt said, "just, uh, interested."

Chattar Lal began to tell the captain that the Thuggee was a mere fabrication of the British who were trying to insult the people of the land they ruled. In fact, he insisted, they had never existed.

Indy's attention drifted away as Chattar Lal went on at great lengths, attempting to prove that the Thuggee was simply myth. Indy didn't want to hear a lot of empty propaganda; he knew for a fact that the Thuggee had existed, had read firsthand accounts of their sinister rituals and evil deeds.

A goblet was set in front of him: the next course. In the goblet sat the head of a monkey, its wide-opened eyes staring at him. The top of its head had been cut off revealing the brains within.

Indy did not recoil in horror. He'd eaten monkey brains before. Really, once a person got over the strangeness of it, it wasn't bad. But before digging in, he looked down the table to see how Willie and Short Round where reacting to this bizarre delicacy.

Short Round's upper lip was quirked up in an expression of utter disgust.

Willie stared, goggle-eyed in disbelief, at the monkey head in front of her.

Indy smiled to himself. He wondered how attractive life in the palace as the wife of a monkey-brain-eating, teenaged maharajah seemed to her now.

Chattar Lal continued to ramble on about how the Thuggee didn't exist and Indiana was growing weary of his lies. Once again, he went straight to the point. "You know, the villagers also told us that Pankot Palace had stolen something very valuable from them."

Chattar Lal reddened angrily. "Dr. Jones, in our country it is not usual for a guest to insult his host," he snapped irritably.

Indy could see he'd struck a nerve. "I'm sorry," he

apologized with feigned sincerity. "I thought we were talking about folklore."

"What exactly was it they say was stolen?" Captain Blumburtt wanted to know.

"A sacred rock."

This revelation was greeted by uproarious laughter from Chattar Lal. "You see, captain," he boomed when he had stopped laughing. "A rock!"

Indy leaned in to Chattar Lal and spoke to him pointedly. "*Something* connected the villagers' rock and the old legend of the Sankara Stones."

He studied Chattar Lal's face for any sign that the man knew about the escaped child who had carried the ancient cloth with him.

Chattar Lal's expression revealed nothing. In fact, his irritable demeanor had vanished and he'd regained his professional, diplomatic equilibrium. His formerly scowling visage was now an inscrutable blank. "Dr. Jones, we're all vulnerable to vicious rumors," he replied lightly. "I seem to remember that in Honduras *you* were accused of being a grave robber rather than an archaeologist."

Chattar Lal had done his homework! "Well, the newspapers greatly exaggerated the story," Indiana commented modestly, undisturbed.

The prime minister stayed on the attack. "And wasn't it the Sultan of Madagascar who threatened to cut your head off if you ever returned to his country?"

Indy chuckled at the memory. "No, it wasn't my head."

"Then your hands, perhaps?" Chattar Lal checked.

"No, it wasn't my hands," Indy assured him, still smiling. He decided not to go on with the true story since it might not seem polite, especially at the dinner table. "It was a misunderstanding."

Chattar Lal threw his hands in the air triumphantly as though Indy had just proved his point for him. "That's exactly what we have here, Dr. Jones — a most unfortunate misunderstanding!"

The young maharajah had been sitting at the head of the table, but had not seemed to be listening to the conversation regarding the Thuggee. At least, that was what Indy thought when he occasionally glanced at him to gauge any reactions he might be having and saw nothing but blankness in the maharajah's expression.

Apparently, though, Indy had been wrong because now the maharajah raised his head and had a very definite opinion. "I have heard the evil stories of the Thuggee cult," he remarked in a mature, even-keeled voice. "I thought the stories were told to frighten children. Later I learned the Thuggee cult was once real and did unspeakable things. I am ashamed of what happened here so many years ago, and I assure you, this will never happen again in my kingdom."

"If I offended you, then I am sorry," Indy told him, and this time the apology was sincere. The maharajah had struck him as an honorable, well-intentioned young man from the moment he began to speak. Indy felt certain that if there was indeed evil at work at Pankot Palace, the maharajah was not the source of it. Of Chattar Lal, he was much less certain.

CHAPTER ELEVEN

*T*hat evening, after the dinner, Indy noticed that Willie and Short Round hadn't been able to eat a single thing. In the excitement of his conversation, he hadn't eaten much either. Fortunately, he was able to get a tray of fresh fruit from a servant. After he and Short Round ate a few apples and oranges, they went up to their rooms with the tray to offer some fruit to Willie. She had claimed she felt sick and had gone straight to her room after dinner.

Sending Short Round to their shared room, Indy knocked on Willie's door. Holding the plate behind his back with one hand, he loosened his bow tie with the other. He wondered if she'd noticed how dashing he looked. When Willie opened the door she was dressed in luxurious purple silk pajamas and a matching robe. Her hair hung loose at her shoulders. "I've got something for you," Indy said.

Her eyes narrowed scornfully. "There's nothing you have that I could possibly want," she replied.

"Right," he said, turning away from the door and shifting the plate of fruit to his front side. He paused long enough to take a loud, crunchy bite from an apple.

Willie was at his side instantly, grabbing the apple from him and voraciously attacking it. "Oh, you're a very nice man," she said as she ate. "Maybe you could be my palace slave."

Willie took the entire plate of fruit from Indy and walked back to her room.

In his room, Indy fumed and paced the floor, only taking a short break to check on Short Round who was sleeping soundly. "Palace slave," he muttered angrily. Who did she think she was? She'd be there knocking on his door in five minutes ... maybe four. But the four minutes, and then five passed, and Willie did not appear. He realized that she really wasn't going to show up. He began to unbutton his shirt to get ready for bed, when he froze. Something inside his room had moved.

It was the male figure in the life-sized wall hanging in the shadowy far corner of the room.

Cautiously, he stepped toward it to get a better look. Perhaps it was just a trick of the torchlight, but he was sure he'd detected movement.

And then, all at once, there was a man standing in the

middle of the room, as if from out of nowhere. He was a very large man dressed in traditional robes and wearing a turban.

The mysterious intruder lifted a yellow silk cord over his head and advanced on Indy.

The Thuggee, Indy thought as his attacker approached and he stepped backwards away from the man. Strangulation was their chosen form of murder and yellow cord was their trademark. It was just as he'd thought! Under other circumstances it would have been gratifying to be right, but that was little comfort at the moment.

The man lunged at Indy and swiftly wrapped the cord around his neck. The huge assassin stood behind him and twisted the cord ever more tightly.

Summoning all his strength, Indy shoved his attacker back against the wall, ramming him hard into it. But the assassin maintained his death grip on Indy's neck.

Gasping for air, Indy snapped up a brass pot from the floor, gripping it by its handle, and, with the last of his strength, smashed it up into the assassin's head with a skull-crashing *clang*.

The assassin reeled back, stunned.

With lightning speed, Indy curled forward and pulled the man into a somersault, sending him flying over his back. Indy's attacker crashed onto the floor and slid next to the bed where Short Round continued to sleep soundly.

All the while, the assassin never lost his grip on the cord around Indy's neck!

The wild, thrashing battle continued right there beside Short Round's bed.

Indy grabbed anything he could reach and hurled it at the assassin. He was so completely involved in this life-and-death battle that he didn't see Short Round awaken and climb out of bed. But the next instant, his young assistant was standing beside him. "Dr. Jones, your whip!" he said, handing the bullwhip to Indy.

Indy grabbed the whip and lashed at the assassin. At last the man released his grip on Indy's throat, allowing Indy to roll to his feet. With another forceful snap, Indy was able to circle the man's neck with the whip's end. Now the tables were turned.

The big man struggled, desperate to pry the whip from his neck, but Indy held fast as his would-be killer gasped for air, his face turning red.

Just as Indy was beginning to feel confident that he'd gotten the best of his enemy, the assassin spun into a full-blown backflip that ripped the whip from Indy's grasp. The Thuggee assassin grinned at him victoriously while the whip handle was still spinning through the air.

His smile came too soon.

The handle of the whip caught in the motor of the slowly spinning fan, and began turning along with the blades. The surprised and horrified assassin was tugged upward like a fish being reeled on a fishing line. The whip twisted around the ceiling fan, pulling him higher and higher until the man's toes dangled off the marble floor. The assassin let out a last dying gasp as he hung from the fan.

Short Round closed his eyes tightly, not wanting to view the awful image of the dead man as the fan slowly spun him in a circle.

"Shorty," Indy said quietly as he slumped onto his bed, rubbing his neck. "Turn off the switch."

Opening his eyes, Short Round obeyed. Instantly the dead assassin dropped to the ground, allowing Indy to uncoil his whip from the fan.

Then he remembered Willie. Was she all right?

He dashed across the hall and burst into her room. She was lying atop her bed, awake. She smiled when she saw him.

But Indy didn't even notice her smile. He was too busy scouring the room. He looked around frantically, swung back curtains, checked under the bed. "There's nobody here," he said.

"I'm here, Indy," she told him, sitting up. "You're acting awfully strange."

Indy knew *she* was there. He was searching for anyone *else* who might be lurking around. He suddenly felt a breeze that ruffled a vase filled with dried flowers. A current of air could mean only one thing — there was some sort of secret passage or cave in this room. He followed the current of air to a statue of a woman in the far corner of the room. Giving it a push back was all it took.

The statue receded into the stone wall and an opening appeared behind it. As soon as Indy stepped through, he became aware of a painted inscription on the inside wall. Spidery Sanskrit calligraphy ran under a flaking illustration of an ancient priest bowing before a god. Indy translated the writing out loud: "Follow the footsteps of Shiva. Do not betray his truth."

Indy took out the piece of cloth he'd received from the escaped boy in Mayapore. The similarities between this picture and the one on the cloth were striking. Both depicted Shiva and Sankara.

Short Round appeared at the open passageway. He looked up at Indy with questioning eyes. "Shorty, go get our stuff," Indy told him. They had some exploring to do.

CHAPTER TWELVE

*I*ndy and Short Round entered the secret passage, moving forward slowly into the inky darkness. "Stay behind me, Short Round," Indy cautioned in a low tone. "Step where I step and don't touch anything."

One of Short Round's best qualities was his ability to follow instructions. But, outweighing this was his overwhelming curiosity about almost everything. Only minutes after Indy warned him not to touch anything, he spied a metal ring on a door embedded in the wall and gave it a forceful tug.

The door shattered!

Two mummified corpses tumbled out, falling onto him.

"HELP!" Shorty shouted.

Indy yanked him out from beneath the rotted bodies. Trembling, Short Round crouched behind Indy. "I step where you step. I touch nothing," he restated Indiana's

warning in a quaking voice. From the way the boy continued to shake, Indy felt certain that this time he'd do as he
was told.

Indy and Short Round continued to creep down
the dark tunnel. Gradually, it grew smaller and Indy had
to duck down to fit. Soon he could hear a crunching
sound underfoot. "I step on something," Short Round
alerted him.

Indy had felt it, too. There had been a definite crunch
underfoot. "Yeah, there's something on the ground,"
he agreed.

"Feel like I step on fortune cookies," Short Round
remarked.

"It's not fortune cookies," Indy said, feeling certain. It
would be much too lucky to be true if they were simply
crunching cookies beneath their feet. He reached into his
jacket pocket and took out a book of matches. "Let me
take a look," he said, igniting a match with his thumb and
watching it flare.

They froze as a gruesome scene was illuminated
around them.

The floor and walls of the narrow tunnel were an
undulating mass of millions of enormous bugs: a living
collection of the world's ugliest arthropods, hexapods, and
arachnids!

Short Round clutched Indiana's arm when he spotted

a huge scorpion on his leg. "That's no cookie," he said in a quivering whimper, pointing to the hideous bug with a trembling hand.

"It's all right. I got it," Indy said, stooping to brush the scorpion off. As he swatted the bug away, another hopped onto him.

And then another!

He batted it off but another two replaced it!

They were jumping on faster than he could get rid of them. In another minute, they would be completely covered.

Indy reached for a bug that was crawling up his shirt when he noticed an open chamber just several yards away. It appeared to be bug-free. "Go! There! Go!" he urged Short Round, steering him toward the chamber.

Short Round wasted no time hurrying into the chamber. Indy followed him. As they entered, Short Round unwittingly stepped on a button in the floor that caused a stone door to roll shut. At the same time, another door at the opposite end of the chamber rumbled closed.

They were trapped inside!

Indy lit another of his matches. The light revealed two skeletons lying on the floor.

Wearing a horrified expression, Short Round began to cross the chamber toward him, but Indy held up a cautioning hand. "Stop," he said. It was better if they stayed still. Who knew what other traps were rigged in this chamber? "Just stand up against the wall, will ya?"

Slowly and obediently, Short Round backed against the wall. "You say stand against the wall, I listen to what you say. Not my fault! Not my fault!"

They had only one hope of getting out of there. And that meant to Indy that their chances weren't too good at all. But he had to try. "Willie!" he shouted through the smallest of openings between the boulder and the door archway. "Willie! Get down here."

When they'd gone into the tunnel, they had left her behind in the bedroom, telling her it was too dangerous for her. Indy was sure they'd travel faster and more safely without her stumbling along and shrieking at every little thing. He certainly had never expected to have to call on her to rescue him. But now he had no choice. "Willie!" he bellowed once again. "Come down here! We're in trouble!"

He waited for what seemed like a long while, though maybe he was just impatient and time was dragging. Finally, off in the distance, he heard a horrified scream and smiled, but only a little.

The scream meant that Willie had come to the crispy corpses Short Round had released from their stand-up crypt. At least she was on her way.

He slid down the wall, preparing to wait for her arrival. She was probably wearing some fluffy heeled slippers and she'd be stumbling along at her own slow pace. *Oh, well*, he thought. The important thing was that she'd heard him calling and was on her way. They were in no hurry.

He had nearly slid to the bottom of the floor when he felt something click against his back. He hoped it was nothing.

It was something.

Instantly, one of the skeletons on the floor jerked to a sitting position as deadly spikes punched up through the floor and started down from the ceiling.

Indy and Short Round began pounding on the doors. "This is serious!" Indy shouted to Willie. "Hurry!"

The ceiling was moving downward!

Soon — he had no idea *how* soon — they would be crushed like bugs in a giant pair of fanged teeth.

What was taking her so long?

Another set of wild shrieks told him that she had reached the hall with all the insects. How tough was she? How much did she care about helping them? He didn't know. He could only hope.

Finally he could hear Willie moving in the tunnel behind the boulder. She hadn't run away, after all! The oil lamp she held flickered into the moving spike-filled chamber.

"There are two dead people down here," she cried, an edge of hysteria in her voice.

"There are going to be two dead people down *in here*!" he said urgently. "Hurry!"

"I've almost had enough of you two," she whimpered unhappily as she came closer.

Indy looked up at the spikes. They didn't have long — and he couldn't be sure Willie would pull through. He needed to do *something*. So when he spotted a skull on the ground, he snapped it up and wedged it firmly between the roller and the track, jamming the mechanism. For a moment, the ceiling slowed its descent and Indy held his breath. With any luck, the gears would lock up and stall the whole thing out. But almost immediately, the skull shattered, sending the ceiling barreling toward them once more. "Willie!" he shouted.

"What's the rush?" she asked as she disgustedly swatted at the many crawling bugs that had attached themselves to her robe.

Indy glanced back at the spikes that were moving ever closer together. "It's a long story," he said quickly, "and if you don't hurry, you don't get to hear it."

She began to pound on the boulder. "Indy, let me in."

"No! Let us out!" Indy didn't have time for this! He was now stooped forward and Short Round clung to his back to avoid the moving spikes.

"Let me in!" she insisted, not realizing what was going on inside the chamber and desperate to escape the crawling bugs. "They're all over me."

The situation inside the chamber wasn't getting any better, and sweat began to bead up on Indy's brow. But he knew that if he started panicking, he'd lose his only shot at getting out of this alive. "There's got to be a fulcrum release lever somewhere," he told her, straining to keep his voice clear and level.

"What?"

"A handle that opens the door," he explained, talking faster. "Go on, look."

"There's no handle," she reported, "Just two square holes."

"Go to the right hole," Indy instructed, his patience wearing thin.

"Hurry, Willie!" Short Round pleaded. A spike now pressed against his forehead, and a look of terror was plastered all over his face.

"Ooohh, there's slime inside this hole," she complained. "I can't do it."

"You can do it," he encouraged her. "Feel inside!"

"*You* feel inside," she objected.

He was out of patience and out of time. "Do it now!" he barked.

"Okay!"

The deadly spikes were nearly poking into Indy's leather jacket. One was pressing down on the brim of his hat. He turned his head sideways and sucked in his breath in one last effort to avoid the spikes.

This was it. "We are going to die!" he shouted, finally losing his cool.

But then he heard the sweetest sound in the world. "Got it!" Willie cried triumphantly.

The spikes suddenly retracted, disappearing into the floor and ceiling, and the stone door slid back into the wall.

Short Round leaped off Indy's back and he slumped against a wall, nearly faint with relief.

Willie raced into the room, still batting bugs off her robe. "Get them off of me! Get them off of me!" she ranted, turning in a frenzied circle. "They're all over me! Get them off! They're all over my body."

She jumped up and down trying to shake off the insects that clung on. As she bent to brush off her legs, her rear end struck the same stone block on the wall that had triggered the trap.

With a rumble, the door rolled back again, sealing the doorway once more, and the spikes began to appear all over again!

"It wasn't me!" Short Round cried out defensively.

Willie screamed, not understanding what was happening.

"Come on! Get out!" Short Round urged, pointing at the rapidly closing door at the other end of the chamber.

"Go! Move! Move!" Indy shouted as they raced for the door.

They got out just in time. *My hat!* Indy thought, realizing that he was bareheaded. Without thinking, he reached back and snapped it up from the floor where it had fallen just seconds before the door crashed shut.

CHAPTER THIRTEEN

*I*ndiana, Short Round, and Willie raced out of the spiked chamber and started down a large tunnel. After a few paces, they were flattened against the wall of the tunnel by a roaring wind that howled eerily like a note of gloomy music.

When it died down, Indy led them around the next curve, toward the light. As he moved forward, the wind howled another dramatic gale that blasted past them just as they reached the mouth of the tunnel.

He stopped suddenly, amazed at the sight in front of him. Willie and Short Round crashed into his back, before they, too, dropped their jaws, astounded by what they were seeing.

Below them, at least five stories down, a colossal subterranean temple had been carved out of a solid mass of rock. A vaulting, cathedral-like ceiling was supported by rows of carved stone columns. Balconies overlooked the temple floor and pillared halls led off to dark side chambers.

And the temple was not empty. Gigantic stone statues of elephants, lions, and scary-looking deities — half-human, half-animal monstrosities with horrible, fanged, leering faces — loomed above crowds of chanting, male worshippers dressed only from the waist down in white loincloths. The rumble of their monotone intonations reverberated against the rock walls around them, making the temple hum as though a steady motor rumbled at its core. They worshipped before an altar jutting from a stone wall in the cavern. Between the worshippers and the altar was a natural crevasse that occasionally spewed clouds of smoke.

At the altar was a statue that towered over all the others. It was similar to the one Indy had found on the road to the palace — the goddess Kali, a manifestation of death and complete destruction.

Unlike the statue at the roadside shrine, this one was even more loathsome. It bore the visage of a hideous, devouring monster, its eyes and fanged mouth dripping blood. Its dangling earrings were made from two human corpses. Many skulls adorned its neck and chest and a gigantic glowing skull sat between its legs. Skulls surrounded its stone feet. Carved serpents twisted up its leg, and around its waist hung a gruesome belt of human hands.

The statue clenched a sword in one of its four arms and a decapitated head of a giant in the other. Its other two hands were stretched forward as if encouraging the adoring throng at its feet, whose chants grew increasingly loud and impassioned.

Willie, Indy, and Short Round watched in silence as three priests in robes materialized out of the swirling smoke. They each carried an urn attached to a strap around their necks. Gray smoke billowed from each urn and they brought it toward the malevolent object of their adoration, the statue of Kali. The priests knelt at the base of the statue and bowed reverently.

"It's a Thuggee ceremony," Indy whispered to Willie and Short Round.

"Have you ever seen anything like this before?" Willie asked quietly.

"Nobody's seen this for a hundred years," he replied.

A huge drum was banged three times.

Abruptly, the chanting ceased.

The silence in the immense chamber was chilling as a sinister figure appeared from out of the smoke. Indy was sure he must be the high priest of the Thuggee cult.

The high priest's red-rimmed eyes glared from sunken sockets in his pale face. His bloodred robes made him look almost as vile and diabolical as the goddess he served. Like her, he wore a necklace comprised of animal fangs and bones. His horned headpiece appeared to have been made from a bison skull on top of which a small, screaming shrunken head had been placed.

The drum banged three more times and the high priest lifted his arms ominously.

From somewhere came a bloodcurdling scream.

All heads turned toward a man dressed only in a loin-cloth, who struggled violently between two priests. They dragged him, screaming and kicking, to an upright iron frame and strapped him in.

The high priest stepped toward his victim and began to intone a wild ritual chant as his hand moved slowly across the man's face and neck.

Suddenly, the high priest placed his hand over the victim's chest, sunk it into the man's body, and removed his living heart.

Willie screamed in horror, clamping her hand over her mouth to stifle the sound and falling back against the rock wall.

Short Round covered his face with his hands, cringing.

Indy felt his stomach lurch. "He's still alive," he murmured to himself quietly, not quite believing his own eyes. But a second glance told him that what he'd witnessed had indeed happened.

The sacrificial victim gazed in amazement down at his

chest, slowly realizing that he was still alive. There was no evidence of a gash on his chest, only a red mark.

As he looked in wonder down at his chest, a stone door beneath him slid open, emitting intense heat along with a rush of steam. The metal frame, on which the victim was chained, was lifted from the ground by a man operating a pulley wheel and directed by one of the priests.

The man looked down into the pit and began to thrash frantically in terror. From where they were standing, high above, Indy, Willie, and Short Round could see what the man was seeing. Molten lava bubbled crimson deep inside the pit!

The priest slowly released the lever controlling the wheel. Willie turned away as the victim was lowered into the molten pit, but Short Round and Indy watched in horror. The lava flared and spit sparks while the screaming man disappeared into it.

The high priest kept the beating heart raised high above his head while this was happening. His eyes were glazed, and the corners of his mouth turned up in a vicious smile. Indy could tell that the man was actually enjoying this!

The metal frame was raised out of the lava pit, glowing red. There was no sign of the man who had been sacrificed.

The fierce wind that had flattened Indy, Willie, and Short Round in the tunnel blew once more. Indy could tell from Short Round's sickened expression that he was appalled by what he'd just seen. His own legs weren't feeling all that sturdy, either, and Willie quivered all over, her face frozen into an expressionless stone mask.

While the multitude of worshippers chanted at a frenzied pitch, the high priest walked back to the altar and disappeared. The three priests approached the altar, each carrying something wrapped in a cloth.

Indy leaned in to get a better look at it.

The priests reverently unwrapped three cone-shaped pieces of crystallized quartz. They placed the three stones in the eyes and mouth below the statue of the goddess. As the stones were brought together they began to glow a burning, incandescent white.

"That's the rock they took from the village," Indy quietly pointed out to Willie and Short Round. "It's one of the Sankara Stones."

"Why do they glow like that?" Short Round asked.

"Shhh," Indy shushed him. If they were discovered here, they'd be in huge trouble. Speaking even more softly, he explained: "The legend says that when the rocks are brought together, the *diamonds* inside them will glow."

"Diamonds?" Willie asked in a whisper.

"Diamonds!" Short Round confirmed with a nod.

They stared down at the altar, mesmerized by the glow from inside the Sankara Stones.

After another moment, the worshippers began to disband, leaving the temple empty. Indy considered that this might be a perfect time to get a better look at what was going on down there. It was too dangerous to bring Willie and Short Round, though. "Look," he whispered to them, "I want you two to stay up here and keep quiet."

"Why? Where are you going?" Willie demanded in a slightly panicked voice.

"Down there," he said as he took the satchel Short Round had packed from the boy. He'd need something in which to carry the stone once he'd gotten back.

"Down there?!" she yelped softly. "Are you crazy?"

"I'm not leaving here without the stones," he told her firmly.

"You could get killed chasing after your fortune and glory," she said, a note of true concern in her voice.

"Maybe," he replied seriously. Then he shot her a grin. "But not today."

Emboldened by her distress, he planted a quick kiss on her lips. Then he swung around to a balcony overlooking the temple.

*   *   *

In the dark shadows of the jumping torchlight, Indy was able to move stealthily along the columns that sat horizontally over the balconies until he arrived at the end.

He peered down at the altar below. If he was going to reach the altar, he would have to find a way to climb down, and then manage to get over the crevasse in front of it.

His eyes darted to a tall column not too far from him, but still at least a yard out of reach. On it a tremendous stone elephant perched, its trunk raised and jutting out past him into the temple.

Mentally he estimated the distance between the balcony, the elephant's stone trunk, and the altar.

After a moment's thought, he decided on a bold and dangerous course of action. It was the only way.

Taking his bullwhip from his belt, he unfurled it, letting its tail drop to his side. Then, with lightning movement, he cracked it, letting it fly. The whip's end wrapped tightly around the elephant's trunk. He tugged the whip taut, took a breath, and jumped.

He swung out on the whip, arching down and over the chasm of fiery lava in a spectacular curving jump, landing lightly on his feet by the altar. Indy rewound the whip and attached it to his belt before moving toward the towering, monstrous statue. At its feet, the three Sankara Stones still glowed.

Indy was aware of their immense power and approached the stones cautiously. Tentatively, prepared to spring back at the first sign of trouble, he reached out and touched one of the stones. Despite its brilliant light, it didn't burn. Carefully, he lifted it, peering into its light, its glow reflected on his face. The diamond glow from deep inside faded as he put the first stone in his satchel and reached for the others.

As he gathered all three stones, he couldn't get over the feeling that the huge, hideous statue above him was watching. Crouching low so not to be seen, he backed away from the statue. Then, suddenly, he heard a voice. Could it be the horrible goddess? No. That was crazy.

The voice was coming from the altar.

Curious, he stepped behind the altar and came upon a column of light emanating from an enormous hole dug below its back. Listening closely, he was sure he heard the clink of metal against rock.

He crept toward the edge of the hole. The light rising up illuminated the horrified expression on his face as he saw what was below him.

Down below was a mine. Concentric paths led off into many narrow tunnels. Crawling around these burrows were scrawny, hollow-eyed children dragging sacks of dirt and rock. Other children pulled the sacks to mine cars waiting on rails.

Straining to lift the rocks into the mine cars, several of the children slipped and fell. Bare-chested Thuggee guards shouted at the enslaved children and kicked some of the ones who had fallen.

Shifting the satchel of stones on his shoulder, he considered what to do next. He could leave with the Sankara Stones now and let the villagers return to fight the Thuggee. It was probably the sensible thing to do.

He couldn't fight all these guards by himself. Could he? Of course he couldn't.

He was distracted from his thoughts by the pleading cry of a child below him. Looking down, he saw a burly Thuggee guard raise his arm and bring it down forcefully on the little slave.

Indy was enraged. What monsters could treat children like this? Anger drove caution from his mind. Indy grabbed a nearby rock and hurtled down at the guard. It crashed onto the shoulder of the Thuggee guard and bounced off, sending him staggering forward.

The startled slave children stared up at him in shock.

The Thuggee guard's head shot up. Indiana met his angry glare with a victorious smile.

His smile faded as he sensed a presence behind him — many presences. Turning slowly, he faced at least a dozen

Thuggee guards, their heads wrapped in turbans. Elaborate designs were painted on their glowering faces, bands of color outlined in white with a broad ring of black circling their eyes.

But what Indy was most aware of were the rifles and the broad, sharp swords gripped firmly in their hands.

CHAPTER FOURTEEN

*A*s Indy stirred to waking, he vaguely recalled being struck on the head by a heavy, blunt object. It hurt to open his eyes, but he had to. In the murky light, he realized he was in a prison cell with his hands chained over his head.

Short Round was chained to wall across the cell from him. "Dr. Jones!" he cried when he saw Indy coming to. He hurried over, his chain clanking behind him, and hugged Indy. "I keep telling you, listen me more, you live longer," he scolded affectionately. Short Round told him that the guards had also captured Willie but that he had no idea where they had taken her.

Indy nodded groggily. Did his head ever hurt! As he came increasingly awake, he noticed a young boy in rags sitting near Short Round. Through the iron bars of the cell he could see children slaving in the mine tunnels.

The boy sat and rocked. He seemed to be praying. "Please let me die," he pleaded. "I pray to Shiva, let me die, but I do not. Now the evil take me."

"How?" Short Round asked him.

"They will make me drink the blood of the evil one. Then I'll fall into the black sleep," he replied.

"What is that?" Indy asked the boy.

"You become like them," he explained. "You are alive — but like a nightmare. You drink blood; you not wake from nightmare."

Guards came and dragged Indy from the cell and chained him once more to a large rock in another chamber of the temple. This one was a terrifying gallery of the monstrous, ritualistic statues and grisly icons of the Thuggee sect.

In one corner there was yet another statue of Kali in her most bloodthirsty form. At the base were the three Sankara Stones the guards had taken back from Indy. Once again, she was draped with necklaces of real human skulls and had a belt that slithered snakes — except this time they were living snakes! Indy felt goosebumps rise on his flesh at the sight of them.

The high priest entered the chamber and walked to

Indy. In person he was even more revolting than he had been at a distance. Without his bizarre headdress, Indy saw the hate burning in his deep sunken, burning eyes.

"I am the high priest, Mola Ram," he introduced himself ominously. "You were caught trying to steal the Sankara Stones." He paused, gazing transfixed at the stones glowing at the statue's feet.

"There were five stones in the beginning," he continued after a moment. "Over the centuries they were dispersed by wars, sold off by thieves like you."

Indy sputtered at the man's audacity. "Thieves like me, huh? Ha! You're still missing two!"

"A century ago when the British raided this temple and butchered my people, a loyal priest hid the last two stones down here in the underground tunnels, the catacombs."

"So that's what you've got these *slaves* digging for, huh?" Indy realized. "They're innocent children!"

A guard entered, gripping Short Round roughly. The boy's eyes were wide with fear.

"They dig for diamonds to support our cause," Mola Ram insisted maniacally. "They also search for the last two stones. Soon we will have all five Sankara Stones and the Thuggee will be all-powerful."

"What a vivid imagination," Indy scoffed.

Mola Ram remained unruffled. "You don't believe me,"

he taunted. "You will, Dr. Jones. You will become a true believer."

The large Thuggee guard Indy had hit with the stone came beside him and loomed there menacingly. Indy winced as he attempted a smile. "Hi," he said as the guard glowered into his eyes.

The boy who had been in the cell with Short Round and Indy entered the chamber. Or was he? Indy felt certain it was the same boy — though he was very much changed. He was now dressed like a Thuggee guard.

More striking than his uniform, though, was his manner. He walked forward, zombie-like, handing Mola Ram a skull. It was the living death he had so feared!

The large guard grabbed Indy's jaw in a crushing grip and jerked his head back. Indy resisted, twisting his head as best he could against the guard's viselike grip.

Mola Ram stood in front of Indiana and tipped the skull forward, attempting to pour the poisoned liquid between Indy's lips. Indy clenched his jaw tightly but a second guard pried it open.

"Dr. Jones, don't drink!" Short Round urged him. "Don't drink! It's bad! Spit it out!"

Blood ran down Indy's chin as, helpless to resist, he had no choice but to let Mola Ram pour it in. He held it in his mouth, gagging, until he couldn't stand it another second and spit it out, spraying Mola Ram and the guards.

Mola Ram gazed down at his clothing and grew furious. As he did this, the young maharajah entered the room. The little prince's eyes glowed angrily and he hissed at Indiana.

Mola Ram spoke to the young maharajah, who stepped in front of Indiana and produced a *kryta* from his robe.

Indy instantly knew what it was. The small doll had been crudely fashioned to resemble him. Like a voodoo doll, it supposedly possessed the power to pass any injury inflicted onto the doll to the person it had been made to resemble.

Ordinarily, Indy wouldn't have been too worried by such a thing, thinking it was only silliness. But he'd already seen the power the Sankara Stones — even the incomplete set — had brought to this cult to dismiss anything. And, as he'd feared, this kryta made him writhe in agony when the maharajah thrust it into a flaming urn.

"Dr. Jones!" Short Round shouted, breaking free of the guard's grip. He jumped up and kicked the maharajah, knocking the boy prince backwards and sending the kryta flying from his hands.

The guards recaptured him instantly, but at least Indy no longer felt the searing heat of the flames.

Mola Ram still seethed with fury. He ordered the guards to turn Indy around and chain him once more against the rock.

The high priest gave orders to the huge guard Indy

had hit earlier. The guard picked up Indy's bullwhip and began to whip him, ripping through his shirt.

After several torturous lashings, Mola Ram approached Indy, the skull of blood in his hands. The guard forced his head back and Mola Ram tipped the skull to Indy's lips.

Mola Ram cackled with fiendish delight. "When the five Sankara Stones are reunited, the Thuggee will rule the world!"

Indiana was horrified by what was happening to him, but so weakened that he was helpless to resist. Still, he tried, clamping his mouth shut. But the guard pinched his nose shut so that he was compelled to open his mouth in order to breathe. The moment his mouth opened, the blood was poured down his throat.

"Dr. Jones," he heard Short Round whisper sadly.

Indy passed out.

When he awoke, Indy found himself on a slab surrounded by hundreds of burning candles. His body convulsed and he groaned in pain as the unspeakable potion took effect.

Then, all at once, his body relaxed. A strange peacefulness came over him. It was unlike any feeling he'd ever had before — being so completely at ease.

He raised his hand and examined it in wonder, as though he'd never really seen it before, never truly realized the power it held.

He was not himself. Dimly, somewhere in a tiny chamber in the back of his mind, he knew this. But, the amazing thing was . . . he didn't care.

He liked this new thing he had become. He smiled malevolently and threw his head back in uproarious laughter.

CHAPTER *FIFTEEN*

*I*ndiana stood before the altar dressed in a loincloth like the other worshippers who chanted to the statue of the goddess. He glanced across the chasm at them. What he had once seen as a sea of frightening faces now seemed like a brotherhood of the Thuggee, all united in their quest to please the goddess they adored.

Chattar Lal, dressed in the robes of a priest, stood beside Indy at the altar. He glanced at the mystical marking on Indy's forehead and his lips quirked in a pinched, approving smile.

The young maharajah sat among the worshippers, but on a raised platform. Like the other believers, the maharajah stared across the crevasse at the altar of Kali.

As he had done before, Mola Ram materialized evilly amidst the swirling smoke coming from the crevasse. Behind him, the three Sankara Stones glowed in the skull beneath the statue's legs. He began to intone in the ancient language of worship, and Indy, staring blankly, translated. "Mother protect us. We are your children. We pledge our devotion with an offering."

He watched, feeling no emotion, as Willie was dragged out, struggling desperately, and dressed in the same beautiful dress she had worn to dinner. But, at dinner, he had been overwhelmed by her loveliness. This time the sight of her did nothing but make him think what a fitting sacrifice she would be.

Chattar Lal turned to Indy. "Your friend has seen and she has heard. Now she will not talk."

The iron frame on which the victim had been sacrificed the day before was brought out. Willie spotted Indy as she was dragged to the frame. "I'm not going to have anything nice to say about this place when I get back," she shouted when the guards pushed her, face first, into the metal lattice.

Craning her head, she looked at Indy questioningly. Why was he just standing there? "Help me, Indy!" she shouted. "What's the matter with you?"

Still chanting in Sanskrit, Mola Ram approached Willie and stroked her cheek. Abruptly, he turned to Indy, who remained impassive, watching Willie struggle.

"Come. Come," Mola Ram commanded Indy.

Trancelike, he began to walk to Willie. "Indy! Help me!" she cried.

Indy just looked away from her terrified face and gazed up adoringly at the statue of the hideous goddess he now served.

Turning back to Willie, Indy stroked her face as Mola Ram had done. "Please snap out of it," Willie pleaded, near tears. "You're not one of them. Please come back. Don't leave me."

She reached out to him with the only hand that was not chained. Indy grabbed her wrist and shackled it to the chain.

"No!" Willie cried, still unable to believe the change in him. "What are you doing? Are you mad?"

Indy responded by calmly closing the outside gate on the iron frame, locking her inside. Outraged, Willie spit in his face. Indy wiped the spit from his face and smiled.

Chains clinked and gears squeaked as the sacrificial frame and its victim were turned facedown and the heavy stone doors slowly opened to reveal the molten death at the bottom of the chasm.

"This can't be happening. This can't be happening," Indy heard Willie telling herself frantically. "Wake up, Willie. Wake up!" But her words did not move him. In his trance, he was there to serve the goddess. That was all he cared about.

One of the priests pushed a lever, and the frame with

Willie strapped to it began to descend slowly into the crevasse. Willie shrieked. "No! No!"

Watching in a passive fog, Indy just stood there and
watched her go. In that small chamber in his mind where
what remained of his old self was trapped, he heard a small
voice urge him to help her, to do something. But the voice
was too far away; he couldn't hear it clearly enough to take
any action.

And then, suddenly, it was much clearer. It wasn't in
his mind, either, but right beside him.

Short Round was there, beside him, tugging on his
hand. Somehow he had managed to escape from the mines
where he'd been imprisoned. "Wake up, Dr. Jones!" he
begged. "Wake up!"

Indy, still in his trance, jerked his hand from Short
Round's grasp, swung it back, and backhanded him, knocking him to the floor.

"Dr. Jones!" he shouted from the floor, tears in his eyes.

Recovering quickly, Short Round jumped to his feet
and ran, pursued by the guards. He grabbed for a torch
and yanked it off the wall. Using it as a weapon, he swung
it at the guards, keeping them at bay as he scrambled over
to Indy.

"Indy, I love you!" he shouted, plunging the flaming
torch into Indy's bare side.

Indy screamed in pain.

"Wake up! Wake up!" Short Round shouted at him urgently.

Indy crumpled to the ground. As he fell, he saw guards rush toward Short Round and grab the torch from him. Another guard moved forward and pulled a knife from his belt.

"You're my best friend!" Short Round cried, in one last attempt. "Wake up, Indy!"

Indy rose slowly from the floor.

He turned to the guards holding Short Round. "Wait!" he told them, holding up a hand. He spoke in the monotone of the zombie-like worshippers. "He's mine." The guards willingly handed Short Round to him and he lifted the boy over his head, carrying him toward the smoking crevasse.

Short Round squirmed in terror. Indy held him out over the opening, gripping him tight.

He looked up into Short Round's terrified face . . . and winked. The boy's voice — and torch — had cut through the smoke befogging his brain and had reached him as no one else could have. "I'm all right, kid," he told him.

Setting Short Round down safely, he whirled and punched an approaching guard. Short Round also sprang into action, stopping another guard with a quick karate kick in the stomach.

Indy heard Willie's screams from down in the fiery pit

of lava. A guard ran to the lever and dropped her farther down. Indy dove for the lever and fought to stop it from descending any more.

Forcing himself to look down into the pit, he saw that the frame had come to stop only yards above the fiery lava. The heat was so intense it scorched him even from the top of the pit. Willie had passed out from fear, dangling unconscious in the extreme heat.

From the other side of the crevasse, the chanting slowly dropped away as the worshippers realized there was a battle taking place on the altar. There wouldn't be much time before Indy and Short Round were swarmed by the hundreds of men in the crowd. If Mola Ram had a way to let them across the crevasse, it would all be over.

It was important to get rid of Mola Ram, he decided. That was their only chance. So Indy grabbed a spear one of the guard's had dropped and charged toward the high priest, shouting his name.

With a triumphant laugh, Mola Ram disappeared through a secret trapdoor near the base of the statue. Seeing his target vanish, Indy tossed the spear aside and threw himself on the wheel controlling the iron frame in the pit. He cranked it furiously and the iron frame began to rise. He continued to strain mightily and before long, Willie appeared at the top of the pit.

But before he could free Willie from the frame, Chattar Lal lunged ferociously at him, pulling a dagger from his sash. He slashed at Indy, forcing him to release the crank wheel as he leaped away from the blade.

With a clank, the frame began to descend once again. And then, with a screech of chains, the frame plummeted deep into the pit.

Chattar Lal slashed again with his dagger, keeping Indy away from the crank.

Indy knew he had to regain control of the crank — and fast — or Willie would not survive. Charging toward Chattar Lal, he kicked the dagger from the man's hand and punched him in the jaw, knocking him backwards.

The gears of the crank slammed to a halt, blocked by Chattar Lal's limp body. In an instant, Indy tossed him off and began furiously winding the gears to pull the frame back up.

Short Round ran to his side, throwing all his weight onto the wheel. Together they labored, and the sacrificial frame with Willie strapped to it came back into view. This time, with Short Round operating the wheel, Indy was able to grab the frame and swing it away from the pit, over the platform. "Give me some slack!" he yelled to Short Round.

Short Round released enough chain for Indy to bring

the frame closer and begin to unstrap the unconscious woman. "Willie, wake up!" he urged her as he worked. "Willie!"

Moaning, Willie moved her head. Indy pulled her off the frame. Her head jerked up and her eyes opened as she began to cough violently. Seeing Indy there, she slapped his face hard.

"Willie, it's me," he told her. "I'm back."

Relief flooded Willie's face when she heard these words and slumped into his arms. "Oh, Indy," she murmured.

The tender moment was interrupted by Short Round, who threw Indy's satchel to him. Turning toward the statue, Indiana grabbed the three glowing Sankara Stones and shoved them inside the bag.

He snapped up Short Round's trusty baseball cap from where it had been knocked off in the struggle and placed it back onto his assistant's head. "Indy, my friend," Short Round said.

The boy reached into his own pants pocket and produced Indy's fedora, the one he'd rolled up and kept for his friend when he'd found it in the prison cell.

"I'm sorry, kid," Indy apologized for all he'd put Short Round through.

Short Round nodded, understanding. "Indy, now let's get out of here."

He held up a hand for Short Round to wait while he peered down into the adjacent mines. Down there he could still see the child slaves working.

Leaning closer, he saw a huge conveyor belt below. Children in chains loaded stones from it onto an elevator that was, in turn, lifted and unloaded by child slaves waiting on a high ledge nearby. They loaded its contents into a mining cart and then one of the children rode the cart down a track and out of sight.

Those empty cars have to go down to the mines, Indy thought. And there had to be a way to get what they found out of the mines without bringing it up through just this one opening. That meant there was a chance he could get down there and find a way to bring all the children out some other way.

There were three of them . . . and hundreds of guards. The plan was completely crazy.

But there were also hundreds of children down there, children desperate to be free.

He thought of the young boy who had made it back to the village. He'd been starved, beaten, and bruised. But his will to return and to help his friends had been so strong that he'd survived. Hundreds of children with that kind of desire could be a powerful weapon.

"Indy," Willie urgently pressed him to get going.

"Right," Indy agreed. But he couldn't leave those children down in that hateful mine. "*All* of us are leaving," he said firmly.

He waved his hand for Willie and Short Round to follow him down to the mines. They would have to lay low and avoid the guards while they searched for the fastest way out.

Willie sighed loudly, but followed Indy and Short Round down. It wasn't very long before they came to a tunnel. Lighting a match, Indy saw a carved door at the end of the tunnel. A dim light filtered through a small window at the top of the door. Indy took in the door's intricate carvings and the quality of the light. *I bet that goes right back to the palace,* he figured.

Willie caught his eye and he knew what she was thinking. They could get out through that door, sneak through the palace, and — if they were lucky — there might be no one in the way to stop them.

In the distance, a whip cracked and a child cried out in torment. Willie looked up at him and nodded. This was a rescue mission now.

CHAPTER SIXTEEN

*I*ndy stood in the shadows of the mining tunnel, watching the child slaves laboring under the watchful eyes of hulking guards and thinking of what to do next. Behind him, Willie and Short Round stayed close to the rock wall, trying to be as invisible as possible. The guard overseeing the nearby group of children was so close that they could smell him.

Indy had a plan — sort of. He had picked the lock of the door leading into the palace using the wire stem of one of the fake flowers on Willie's gown. It was now unlocked, a clear escape route, just waiting.

But that was as far as his plan went. How he was going to free these children under the noses of the guards was something he hadn't quite figured out — but he was working on it.

Something would come to him. It always did.

A small girl fainted to the ground and the other children

frantically urged her to get up before the guards noticed her. Clearly, they had seen the awful fate awaiting any worker who fainted. Alerted by the clamor of their voices, a burly, guard turned and glared at the fallen girl. He strode toward her and raised his whip to strike.

This was more than Indy could bear.

Plan or no plan, he couldn't let this brutality happen right in front of him. Stepping out of the shadows, infuriated, he flattened the guard with one mighty blow to his jaw.

A low gasp swept through the group of startled children. One small boy dared to cheer, which immediately set off a torrent of happy shouts.

Willie and Short Round scrambled out from hiding as the rebellious slave children swarmed around Indy, their chains clanking. Willie lost no time in finding the large gold key in the guard's jacket. In minutes, she became busy unlocking the shackles that held the children prisoner, while Indy and Short Round made quick work of pulling off their chains, which rattled as they fell to the ground.

Not long after that, the liberated kids spilled from the tunnels where they'd been imprisoned for so long. Indy directed them toward the tunnel that would lead them out of the mines and into the palace.

As they stampeded, they knocked over any of the guards that tried to stand in their path, their sheer numbers allowing the children to easily trample right over them. Looking down from a ledge, another group of kids waited with baskets of rocks. When an ascending squad of guards approached underneath them, they overturned their baskets, instantly disabling them.

Indy, Willie, and Short Round searched every fallen guard they found for more keys. Indy kept any of the guards that tried to rise in place with more well-aimed punches to the jaw. Soon they had enough keys to pass out to the freed children, who moved quickly to unlock the shackles holding more of their friends.

The swarm of excited, joyful children made it all the way aboveground to the top of Pankot Palace and exploded into the pavilion where Indy, Willie, and Short Round had dined earlier.

They ran across the banquet table and kicked aside the luxurious cushions around it. Now they could see the windows — and the light — that showed them the way out.

Yelling with happiness, they burst out the front doors into the glorious, bright sunshine that they had not seen for such a long time.

Indy, Willie, and Short Round unlocked child after child until the last one was out. Willie had just freed the last small girl, sending her scampering to meet her brother's waiting hand when a very large Thuggee guard barreled down the tunnel toward them with a raised club in his hand and a mean, determined expression on his face.

Whirling to face him, Indy grabbed a nearby sledge-hammer from the ground and hit the giant man in the stomach. The guard didn't seem to feel it. He wrenched the hammer out of Indy's hands and flung it away.

The Thuggee lifted Indy over his head as if he were no more than a doll. He slammed Indy into a mine car and then doubled him over with a blow to the stomach.

As he slid down the side of the car, he was aware that Willie was off to the side arguing with Short Round, trying to keep him out of the fight. "I gotta save him!" Short Round protested as she clutched his shoulder, holding him back from going to Indy's aid.

"He can take care of himself," she insisted, though she didn't sound entirely convinced.

As Indiana struggled with the guard, he wasn't entirely sure he could get the best of this fight, either. Suddenly, mysterious, piercing pains were shooting up and down his legs. And he was short of breath, as though his chest was being squeezed by a giant hand. Although he swung at the guard, his blows fell lightly, without sufficient force to slow the man down.

Short Round could see that Indy was losing the struggle. What was happening to Indy? He wanted to rush in and help, but Willie was holding tight to his shoulders.

Indy was grateful, and hoped she would be able to maintain her grip. Even with Short Round's spunk and all his good intentions, he didn't stand a chance against the giant of a man who was now pummeling Indy.

"He needs me!" Short Round shouted at Willie, still struggling to get free. "I gotta save Indy!"

The Thuggee guard lifted Indy once again, and spun in a circle with Indy over his head two times. Indy's strength had left him completely. He had no way to free himself when the guard turned to the mining car, about to heave Indy into it.

He looked over to Willie and Short Round helplessly, his face creased with an apologetic expression. The guard would turn his attention to them next, and there was nothing he could do about it now. He was failing them and he felt terrible about it.

He locked eyes with Willie. Her jaw dropped slowly as she realized how helpless he really was. "Okay, save him," Willie relented, letting go of Short Round.

Short Round grabbed a whip from one of the fallen guards and began to lash at the legs of the man holding Indy. "Drop him down!" Short Round insisted fiercely, still wielding his whip. "I kill you! Drop him down!"

The guard dropped Indy into the cart and scooped up Short Round instead. The boy screamed and kicked out at his Thuggee attacker, but just as Indy had predicted, he was no match for him. The large man easily tossed Short Round aside, sending him sliding along the rock floor of the cavern until he stopped beside a pool of water, nearly hitting his head on a pulley system that had been used to bring water up to the mining level high above.

When Short Round stopped sliding, a noise caught his attention and he looked up. The sound was coming from a rock balcony on the upper level, overlooking the cavern below.

On the balcony stood the malicious young maharajah — and in his hand he held the kryta doll made to look like Indy. He was staring intently, stabbing the replica doll repeatedly with a long, sharp, sapphire-tipped turban pin.

Although he was dizzy from banging his head on the edge of the cart, Indy climbed to stand once more. Gripping the sides of the cart for support, he followed Short Round's gaze and witnessed the maharajah stabbing the doll.

Indy had felt the power of this doll earlier. No wonder he couldn't fight!

Short Round leaped out over the pool, grabbing onto the big water bucket attached to chains on the pulley mechanism just as it was rising with a bucket full of water. Clinging to the bucket, he sailed upward.

Indy was distracted from watching Short Round when

the guard jumped into the cart and began pounding him with a hammer-like fist. They fought fiercely, every blow rocking the cart. They slammed against its side, their combined weight finally tipping it over and dumping them onto the wide conveyor belt behind the mining cart. All around them, large rocks were being carried somewhere by the moving belt. Their struggle continued as the belt moved them along with the rocks to some unknown final destination.

Indy threw himself into the struggle. He was dimly aware of someone running alongside of the conveyor belt. A quick glance told him it was Willie.

But he didn't have long to look: His head was roughly jerked back around. The guard's hands closed around his throat, repeatedly banging his head against the conveyor belt. Indy couldn't breathe and didn't have the strength to break the Thuggee's choke hold on his windpipe. Now he was sure that the kryta doll was the reason for his weakness.

Willie had found a heavy, metal bucket. "Here! Try this!" she shouted, pushing the bucket onto the conveyor belt beside the flailing, breathless Indy. Snapping it up, he hit the bucket over the guard's head with a resounding clang.

The guard reeled back, his eyes momentarily blank.

Indy was able to kick the guard away and scramble to his knees. But instantly, a piercing pain ran up his spine, crippling him and causing him to fall back onto the conveyor. *Get that doll, Shorty*, he thought desperately as he writhed in agony.

A loud pounding sound was coming closer to him now. What was it?

It was agonizing for him to strain around backwards to get a look, but he had to do it. Just about two yards further on, tiny pebbles sprayed through the air.

The conveyor belt carried its contents to a large, heavy, stone wheel. The rocks on the conveyor belt were being smashed to smithereens by a rock-crushing machine! If Indy didn't find a way off, he'd be next.

But the sharp pain in Indy's back made it impossible to move. All he had to do was throw himself off the conveyor belt to avoid becoming dust, but even that small movement was more than he could manage.

Nearby, the guard had rallied and was crawling toward Indy on the conveyor belt. If the guard didn't finish him off, the rock crusher would do the job!

Suddenly, the pain in Indy's back and legs stopped. Breath rushed into his lungs with a bracing whoosh of air. His normal strength and agility came roaring back.

Indiana knew what had happened: Short Round had gotten the kryta doll away from the maharajah.

And just in time!

The giant Thuggee guard was now looming over him, and the rock crusher was no more than three feet away. Indy didn't waste any time. He grabbed the nearest thing he could: a handsaw he glimpsed beside the conveyor. It wouldn't be his first choice of weapon, but it'd have to do. He swung with all his strength, hitting the guard directly in the stomach.

The guard staggered backwards and collapsed in front of the rock crusher. Coming to his senses, he rolled over, attempting to scurry away on his hands and knees, but it was too late. The long sash of his uniform was already caught! As the guard screeched in horrified terror, he was pulled into the crushing wheel!

Indy turned away, unable to watch the guard's horrific death. Then he climbed up onto a catwalk that hung above the conveyor belt. He had to make sure Short Round was safe.

It wasn't long before he caught sight of the boy trading punches with the young maharajah on the balcony. Indy picked up his pace. It looked as if Short Round could use some help.

A Thuggee guard appeared on the walkway in front of Indy, blocking him. But this time, Indy was full of restored energy and quickly flattened him with a powerful blow.

Looking back toward the fight, he watched helplessly

as the maharajah had pulled out a knife and was lunging for Short Round. Indy knew he would never reach Short Round in time to stop him.

Short Round was backed up against the wall, with nowhere to go. But he was used to tight corners, and still had a few tricks up his sleeve. During their fight, there was something in the maharajah's blank gaze that Shorty recognized. Thinking quickly, he reached for the burning torch hanging on the wall above and hit the maharajah with it, just as he had done to Indy.

The effect was the same!

The cloudiness in the maharajah's eyes lifted. He looked as though he was awakening from a long sleep. He shook his head, gazing around and obviously perplexed at finding himself in such unfamiliar surroundings.

"It was the black sleep," Short Round told him.

Indy swung onto the balcony just in time to see the maharajah wake. *Well, that explains a lot.* Indy had a good feeling about the young ruler when they'd first met, and his instinct didn't often lead him astray. He couldn't be angry with the maharajah now; not when he himself had fallen under the sinister spell.

"Shorty, quit fooling around with that kid," Indy joked as he dropped to the balcony floor.

"Okay dokey, Indy," Short Round agreed with a happy grin.

He'd made light of the situation, but they really did have to move quickly. They had won this battle, but who knew how many they had left to fight? Hundreds of Thuggee guards still stood between them and freedom.

"Please, listen," the young maharajah said. "To get out, you must take the left tunnel."

CHAPTER SEVENTEEN

*S*hort Round and Indy made their way along the catwalk, headed down to the lower level of the cavern to reach Willie. They'd already spotted her in the cavern below, pushing a mining car along a rickety track, trying to get it rolling.

Smart, Indy thought as they ran along the catwalk to her. A mining cart would be the fastest and most direct route out of this diabolical pit.

Suddenly Mola Ram and six Thuggee temple guards ran out onto a high platform next to an underground waterfall. At a shouted command from their leader, two of the guards pulled out pistols and opened fire.

Ducking and rolling, Indy and Short Round dodged the bullets as they made their way forward. The guards stopped shooting only when the remaining four guards appeared on the catwalk.

Indy stepped in front of Short Round to protect him. His fist flew in a blur of activity. Short Round kicked and pounded every guard who fell in his path.

A guard slashed at Indy with a sword, slicing the air with rapid movements. Indy ducked as the sword came down inches from his shoulder and sunk into the wooden railing of the catwalk. While the guard frantically attempted to yank the sword out of the railing, Indy slammed his knee up into the guard's stomach and then brought his fist down onto his neck.

From their high vantage point on the catwalk, Indy could see guards hurrying toward Willie. He nudged Short Round and pointed to a rope that reached all the way down to where Willie was still struggling with the cart and jerked his thumb, silently indicating that he wanted Short Round to go down and help her.

Short Round did as Indiana instructed, deftly leaping the short distance from the catwalk to the rope. When he was at the floor, Indy saw more guards running forward on the catwalk. "Shorty! Quit stalling!" he yelled down to the boy.

Willie had gotten the cart to a slow roll and was struggling to get into it. A guard was now racing after her. Short Round would have to be faster than the guard in order to catch up with Willie and get into the cart.

"Go! Go!" he urged Short Round as he ran toward the cart.

The cart was picking up speed. Indy wasn't sure Short Round could run fast enough to reach it. With his eyes darting back and forth between the guards approaching him on the catwalk and Short Round, the guards, Willie, and the rolling cart below, Indy knew he'd have to do some fast thinking and quick, tough fighting if they were going to get out of this one.

The guard below ran faster to get hold of Willie in the cart. With a reckless burst of energy, he leaped forward and grabbed hold of the cart's side. Willie screamed and held onto the cart's other side as the guard tried to climb in with her. But the cart had gained more speed and was moving too fast for the guard to get in. Instead, he was dragged along, refusing to let go, his legs trailing behind him.

More guards were gaining on Short Round, closing in from behind. "Shorty! Look out!" Indy shouted down to the boy. If he didn't get on that cart with Willie soon, the guards would overtake him.

Short Round had reached Willie's cart, where the guard was still being dragged along behind it. Moving as fast as his short, sturdy legs had ever carried him, he raced up the guard's legs, over his back and shoulders, and into the cart!

Even though the Thuggee guard was *still* clinging to the cart, it had begun to roll down an incline and was picking up speed at an even faster rate. It would soon outpace all the other guards. But it was the best chance of escape, and if Indy didn't do something quickly, it would speed away from *him*, as well.

He was only yards away from the end of the catwalk and guards were still coming forward, grinning satisfied smiles, sure he was trapped there. His eyes darted around, searching for some escape route and not finding any.

Out in the middle of the ceiling, a block and tackle crossbar hung balanced on a long rope. It had been used to transport rocking and mining equipment across the wide expanse of cavern. Could it transport Indy, too? It was a crazy plan, but Indy thought he just might be able to jump out far enough to reach it.

No. It was too far. If he jumped and missed, there was nothing out there but air. He would hurtle to his death on the cavern floor below.

The approaching guards were nearly to him. He glanced at them and back to the block and tackle. *It's too nuts*, he decided.

But what other choice did he have? He was a dead man once these guards reached him.

When the approaching guards were just a yard away, he took off running . . .

"Come on, Indy!" Short Round urged from the cart.

"Hurry!" Willie called.

"Hurry! Hurry!" Short Round agreed frantically.

. . . and leaped into the wide, open expanse of cavern.

Bullets whizzed past Indy as he sailed, like a parachute jumper with no chute, toward his goal.

The bar of the block quickly came closer. With a thud, one hand grasped half the bar, but his dangling weight upset the balance and pulled his fingers toward the edge. One finger slipped, then another, and suddenly, there were only three fingers between Indy and certain death.

Arms and legs flailing wildly, he kicked and reached forward with his other hand.

At last — a solid grip. Now propelled by Indy's weight, the block and tackle began to move. He was traveling on a downward path along the rope toward the speeding mining cart carrying Willie and Short Round, as well as the guard still tenaciously clinging to its back.

But Indy's troubles weren't over. He quickly discovered that the bar was greasy and hard to keep hold of. He pulled himself up with all his strength, struggling to get the bars under his arms as he hurtled forward at incredible speed.

But in moments, he was directly over the cart. He let go of the bar, dropping three body-lengths down, joining Willie and Short Round with a crash.

In this part of the mine, the tracks caused the cart to

swerve sharply around the curving cavern walls. Above and below them, the wooden tracks crisscrossed one another like an elaborate roller coaster ride.

Indy couldn't believe the guard was still holding on, but there he was, trying desperately to pull himself into the cart. *This is where you get off,* Indy thought as he gave the guard a push.

Shouts from behind alerted him that six rifle-wielding guards had jumped into another mining cart and were now chasing them, speeding down the track behind their cart. Short Round and Willie ducked low as the bullets flew.

At the same time, Mola Ram led another squad of armed guards out onto a rock ledge and ordered them to open fire.

Up ahead, Indy saw that the tracks split into two paths. One led back into the quarry and the other led out of the mine.

Indy saw a switch on the rock wall rapidly approaching. At the bottom of the cart, a shovel sat beside a rotted, old railroad tie. Thinking fast, he grabbed the shovel and, gripping its handle, he held it out toward the switch and braced for impact.

CLANG!

He hit the switch!

The cart was shunted, tipsy-turvy onto the track toward the two tunnels, racing away from the guards in the other cart. Willie cringed, her eyes shut as they barreled toward the tunnel — the right tunnel.

"Indy, it's the left tunnel!" Short Round shouted, recalling the maharajah's words. "The left tunnel, it should be the *left* tunnel!"

Willie clutched Short Round as the mine cart picked up speed and roared around a curve at top speed. Wind rushed past them and it was growing ever darker.

It was too late to do anything about taking the left tunnel now. They were speeding back into the quarry.

Chapter EIGHTEEN

*I*n the blackness of the quarry, Indy pulled back on the brake lever to control the cart's speed and keep it from careening off the tracks. Watching for trouble, Short Round peered over the back side of the cart.

Willie ducked, looking up as the dangerously low beams passed over their heads. Then she groaned with dread when the cart plummeted on a steep track, descending even deeper into the quarry.

A gunshot rang through the pitch blackness. Indy whirled away from its whistling song. Once his eyes had adjusted, Indy could see the black form of another cart filled with Thuggee guards swinging around a curve behind them. "We've got company!" Indy warned Willie and Short Round.

Mola Ram's gunmen had spotted them, too. They began blasting away. Bullets ricocheted erratically off the mine walls.

Short Round scurried forward beside Indiana and took hold of the brake, freeing Indy to battle the guards. "Let it go," Indy instructed Short Round.

"What?" the boy questioned, not understanding.

"Let it go!" Indy told him. Short Round didn't move, so Indy released the brake himself. The cart rocketed forward at an unbelievable velocity. "It's our only chance to outrun them," Indy shouted, gripping the side of the cart so hard his knuckles ached.

They all shouted in terror as, there in the blackness, they hit a curve so sharp that it tipped the cart precariously to one side.

The curve was so extreme and they were hurtling around it so fast that the inside wheels lifted off the track! Indiana was thrown to the bottom of the cart. Willie and Short Round tipped over, too, tumbling onto him.

Peering up over their heads into the darkness, Indy saw that the guards behind them had also taken off the brake and were racing down the track at top speed. "Shorty!" Indy said.

"Huh?" he asked.

"Take the brake. Watch it on the curves or we'll fly right off the track."

"Okay," Short Round agreed as gunfire continued to explode all around them.

As the cart dropped back onto two wheels with a thud, Indy felt for the railroad tie he recalled seeing at the bottom of the cart. Getting to his knees, he heaved the heavy beam onto the back of the cart. Then, he stood, and with a great effort, pushed it over the edge of the cart and onto the tracks.

The gunmen behind them spotted the beam in their path and began to cry out in panicked alarm.

The cart hit the beam with a roaring crash. The guards screamed horribly as the car tumbled end over end, slamming against the tunnel walls, and sending pieces of metal, wheels, and other debris shooting in every direction.

Willie and Short Round whooped with joy, but it was short-lived. More gunshots rang out and a second mining cart full of gunmen appeared behind them.

The walls of the tunnel flashed past and curves appeared in the darkness as the top-speed chase continued. Indy staggered to standing, clutching the shovel.

"What are you doing?" Willie asked in a fearful shout.

"Short cut!" he replied.

"What, Indy?" Short Round asked uncertainly.

"Short *cut*!" Indy repeated, once again reaching out with the shovel for a switch in the rock wall.

The guards behind began shooting at Indy. Their bullets clattered off Indy's outstretched shovel blade, making it nearly impossible to hold steady. Despite the gunfire, he concentrated on reaching the switch, batting the shovel blade at it as they whizzed past.

The car abruptly swerved onto a new track, throwing them all to one side.

A bullet clanged off the switch, throwing it back and diverting the guards' cart onto another, parallel track. The guards that had been behind them were now able to come alongside, raising their rifles to shoot.

Indy reached out and grabbed hold of one rifle, attempting to pull it from the guard's hand. Behind him, another guard reached forward, grabbing hold of Short Round, lifting him off his feet. Indy dropped his grip on the rifle and clutched Short Round's legs, working hard to prevent the guard from pulling Short Round into his own cart.

"Indy! Help!" Short Round hollered as he was yanked in two directions as the carts continued to career along the two, side-by-side tracks. "Indy!"

"Pull him in!" Willie shouted, joining Indiana in pulling Short Round back inside the speeding cart.

Ahead, a rock divider threatened to split Short Round in two. If they didn't pull him back in the next minute, Indy and Willie would be forced to release Short Round to avoid killing him.

As the rock divider raced toward them, Indy gave a powerful tug and pulled Short Round into his arms. The shaking boy wrapped his arms around Indy, quaking with terror.

At the divider, the both tracks rose dramatically higher and divided, so that the track the guards were on now ran above the one Willie, Indy, and Short Round rode. Peering over the side of the cart, Indy realized exactly how far above the chasm they were, the tracks held up by wooden supports that looked serviceable, but not sturdy. They certainly weren't meant to take the abuse of a high speed chase, he realized grimly.

They could hear the cart carrying the Thuggee guards rumbling above them. Indy thought hard, trying to calculate where the tracks might meet again. He didn't want to have to fight off a cart running alongside as they just had. It seemed to him that they might actually be in the clear. The track had no doubt divided to carry the carts riding on it to a different destination.

There was no way the guards could get to them now. Unless . . .

Well, there *was* one way — but he didn't believe they'd have the nerve to do it.

As if answering his challenge, one of the guards dropped down into their cart, and immediately grabbed hold of him. Willie screamed.

He had been wrong. Obviously, they did have the nerve.

The two men grappled with one another, struggling desperately. Indy knocked the man to the floor of the cart, but he instantaneously reappeared behind him, clutching Indy in a strong choke hold.

But this guard had underestimated the other passengers in the cart. Willie jumped into the fight and punched him in the jaw. He lost his grip on Indy as he flew up and over the front of the cart and tumbled off the track.

Indy turned to thank her, but his words caught in his throat. Just a couple hundred feet away, the track ended — there was a gap at least five car lengths long!

He pushed Short Round and Willie to the cart's floor and then knelt beside them as the cart flew off the track, sailing out into the air.

Would it make it?

They all cringed, hunched down in the cart, not daring to look over the sides, while the cart hurtled forward carried by nothing other than its own momentum.

BANG! The front wheels hit the other side of the track. Indy felt as though his bones were shaking and his teeth were rattling in his mouth. Then the back wheels took hold.

Yes! he thought with a long, low sigh of relief.

But suddenly, the cart began wobbling crazily. Looking down, they saw what was causing it. Mola Ram was down below with his men. The men banged at the track's wooden supports with large sledgehammers. They were trying to knock the track down and they appeared to be succeeding!

And that wasn't even the worst of it. Across from the track, an immense water tank sat on high wooden supports. They were also banging at those supports. If that tank went over, it would flood the tunnels.

Willie gripped Indy's arm as, together, the three of them saw the gigantic tank begin to list forward and topple toward the ground. The noise was deafening when it hit, sending a half million gallons of water exploding across the cavern and surging in a tidal wave toward the tunnels.

The cart continued its mad pace along the tracks. They were going so fast that Indy worried that they would fly off the tracks. "Brake," he told Short Round, who was standing beside the hand brake.

"Okay?" Short Round replied, pulling on the brake with all his weight. But it didn't slow the cart. His face crunching and reddening with effort, he pulled on it even harder. The increased force snapped the break lever completely off the cart. Short Round fell backwards, still clutching the busted lever. "Uh-oh! Big mistake! Big mistake, Indy!" he shouted.

"Figures," Willie muttered despondently, dropping her head into her hands and shaking her head. This only lasted a moment — right away, the cart tossed her across the floor. Pulling herself up onto its side, she held on for dear life.

Indy crawled toward Shorty and bent over the front of the cart as it pitched to the right and began a screaming decline into a section where the tunnel widened. He could see the brake hanging loose on the outside of the cart, so he swung himself over the front side of the cart and lowered himself as carefully as he could.

He clung onto the outside of the hurtling cart, bouncing along just inches above the rail. To him, the sparking track below his feet was no more than a blur passing beneath as he attempted to kick the brake pad back up.

And then his foot slipped! His hand clenched the side more tightly then ever as the cart dragged him along, his feet kicking the track.

With all the strength he could summon, he forced his leg from the track and felt around the undercarriage of the cart, searching for a foothold. He found one, which steadied his position a little. With his other foot, he resumed kicking the brake as hard as he could.

After five solid slams, the brake finally moved forward against the front wheel, slowing its forward motion. The wheels screeched as they rubbed against the brake. "We're still going too fast!" Willie shouted.

"Help!" Short Round bellowed.

Groaning with the effort, Indy shoved his boot against the wheel, trying to create even greater friction. Small sparks were forming under his heel and he could smell smoke.

Seeing the look of horror on Willie's face, he followed her gaze, quickly checking over his shoulder. The track ended in about fifteen yards! Beyond it was nothing but rock wall.

He *had* to slow this cart down!

Bracing himself on the cart, he applied even more pressure to the brake. The bottom of his shoe felt warm and he could smell the rubber of his soles melting, but he couldn't let up.

He wasn't sure if he was imagining it. Was the cart slowing? It seemed like it might be.

It was slowing!

But would it be enough to keep them from crashing?

The cart rolled to a stop just inches from the rock wall, pressing Indy's back up against it.

He'd done it! Gulping for air, he laughed out loud with relief. But looking down, he realized that smoke billowed up from his shoe.

"Water!" he shouted as he stomped his foot on the ground. He'd created so much friction that his shoe had ignited! There was a fire inside it, searing the bottom of his foot. "Water! Water!"

"Oh, you're on fire!" Willie shouted, both sympathetic

and frantic, as she hopped around him helplessly, not knowing what do. Where could she find water? Instead, she kicked dirt on his shoe in an attempt to smother the flame.

The dirt helped and as his pain abated, Indy slowly became aware of an ominous rumbling, getting steadily louder. Whatever was causing it was coming toward them with great velocity.

When he looked toward the sound, he froze, paralyzed with fear, yet awestruck at the sight before him. They'd survived a lot, but this had to be the end. How could they survive this?

A monster wall of water crashed spectacularly around a turn in the tunnel. This tidal wave had been unleashed when the Thuggees dumped the water tank, and it had only picked up power as it rushed through the tunnels. Now it had finally reached them. It was as though a veritable tsunami struck the tunnel walls, spewing foam and debris: an unstoppable juggernaut.

"Come on! Come!" Indy shouted, gripping Short Round by the wrist. The three of them ran faster than they'd ever moved in their lives.

The tidal wave smashed forward, booming behind them, and Indiana knew this was a race they were bound to lose.

Just then, he spotted a narrow opening in the tunnel

wall. If it led nowhere, the water would fill it and they'd drown then and there. But if it led to the outside . . .

It was a chance they'd have to take because they would never be able to outrun this crushing flood of racing water. He pulled Short Round in front of him, and shoved him into the hole. Then he steered Willie into it as fast as he could, quickly following them into the black space.

They pressed their backs against a cold wall and watched as the colossal tidal wave exploded past the opening, drenching them with its spray.

The roar of the rushing water subsided slightly and they caught their breath, panting hard, but once again relieved to be alive.

Their rest was cut short almost instantly by the sound of a loud bang. The force of the water had pushed the wave into this opening and it was once more cascading toward them relentlessly at torrential speed.

"Let's go!" Short Round hollered. They all took off, yelling with fear, down this new tunnel that led to who knew where.

As the tidal wave loomed up to annihilate them, a small speck of blue appeared ahead of them. New hope sprang up inside Indy.

A way out!

If they could only outrun the rushing tidal wave behind them!

Cold spray pelted the back of his neck as they raced toward the ever-brightening sunlight.

Willie was the first to reach the end of the tunnel — and she let out a bloodcurdling scream. Indy reached her a second later, with Short Round still in his grip. He and Short Round also let out cries of terror.

Flailing their arms wildly, the three of them faltered, trying desperately not to lose their balance.

They had come out onto the sheer face of a cliff. They teetered there precariously, looking down in horror at a three-hundred-foot drop to a gorge of foaming water below.

CHAPTER NINETEEN

Swinging her arms, Willie lost her balance and began to pitch forward. Indy grabbed her, hurling her to his left onto the narrowest of ledges. He moved Short Round beside Willie just before stepping over onto an even narrower rock shelf on the right of the opening.

He'd barely gained a sure footing when an explosive torrent of water burst from the tunnel. The gusher spewed forth, sending rock and debris from the cliffside into the air.

The erupting, pressurized geyser slammed a log out through the opening in the cliff face near Indy's head. Willie screamed as another log slammed through right beside her.

"Willie! Look out!" Short Round shouted.

The ledge beneath her feet was crumbling, shaken by the eruption of water.

She moved in tiny, frightened sideways steps to a place where the crumbling rock was more solid. Looking down the steep and towering precipice, she flattened her back to the rock wall and stared skyward, terrified by the view below.

They couldn't afford to stay there long. Eventually, one of them would slip. It was only a matter of time, Indy thought, knowing that he couldn't let panic get to him. Despite the cascading water at this side and the dizzying drop below, he forced himself to survey the situation as rationally as possible, scanning the vast rock for any sort of escape route that might present itself.

A surge of new hope grabbed him as he spotted a long, narrow, rope bridge that crossed to a cliff on the other side spanning the gorge below. It was about six yards to the left of Willie and Short Round and twenty feet above them. The gusty wind made it swing back and forth. Crossing it would be harrowing, but it beat their only other alternative, which was to go straight down.

To reach the bridge they would have to traverse the narrow ledge very slowly, one tiny footstep at a time, and with the utmost caution climb the sheer face of the cliff. And more dangerous still, in order to get to it, Indy would have to find a way to cross the blasting torrent of water still spraying from the opening at full force.

"Head for the bridge!" he shouted across the water to Willie and Short Round.

Willie's head snapped to her left and then back to

Indy, her eyes wide with terror at the idea of moving even one more step. Nonetheless, she glanced at Short Round who had begun to move and crept along behind him, her back flat against the rock wall.

Drawing in a deep breath to steady his nerves, Indy turned to face the wall and dropped down so that the length of his body was below the cascading water. Painstakingly, he went from foothold to handhold to foothold, inching along under the spray until he reached the other side.

The thundering water was deafening and the further underneath it he went, the more his hands slipped and slid. He couldn't allow himself to think about what he was doing, the insane danger of it, only to consider where he might position his hands and feet next. He clung to pieces of soaked scrub brush jutting from the cliff and rested for the briefest of seconds on small outcroppings along the way.

Finally, he made it out of the water and pulled himself up onto the ledge where Willie and Short Round had stood. In a short time, he had crept along the narrow ledge and would soon join them at the bridge.

He could see them ahead, viewing the bridge with apprehension. He knew it was far from reassuring. The ropes that made up the bridge crossing the gorge must have been years old, perhaps even dating back to the original glory of Pankot Palace. Lying across the two bottom rope spans, worm-eaten and rotten boards offered risky footings. Vertical side ropes attached to the long horizontal pieces of old rope were all they would have for hand railings.

Short Round stepped out bravely onto the bridge with a small bounce. It held him. He turned to Willie with a smile. "Strong bridge," he told her encouragingly. He made another light bounce just to prove his point. "Come on. Let's go. Strong bridge."

Willie didn't budge, so Short Round bounced even harder. "Look! Strong wood! Come on!"

Suddenly, with an anguished wail of terror, he fell through the board, clinging desperately with his hands onto the bridge. "I'm falling down!" he screamed, his legs kicking.

"Shorty!" Willie cried with a gasp.

Indy quickened his steps, hurrying to reach Short Round, but he couldn't run or he would lose his footing. All he could do was to keep moving forward steadily and not let the boy's horrified squall unnerve him.

"Help! I'm falling down! Help! Help!" Short Round continued screaming.

In the water below, hungry crocodiles thrashed expectantly, eyeing the delicious morsel dangling far above their heads.

Willie crawled toward Short Round on hands and knees and gripped his arms firmly at his shoulders, slowly pulling him back up onto the bridge. "Not very funny," Short Round whimpered, his body aquiver.

Willie held him tightly until his trembling subsided. Then the two of them cautiously set out to cross the bridge, picking their way carefully and assessing the strength of each board before putting a foot down on it. Their job was made no easier by the bridge's constant swaying and heart-stopping up and down movement.

Indy watched their progress as he neared the entrance to the bridge. He was about to step onto it to follow them, when a sound caused him to glance back over his shoulder. Two Thuggee guards were rushing toward him. Yelling savagely, they swung their swords in an elaborate attack pattern.

Indy reached for the holster at his side, wanting to grab his gun, but found that it was empty. The guards were on him in seconds, flashing their swords and shouting.

Indy began to throw punches as rapidly as he could. He hit the first guard and ducked under his sword, grabbing him from behind and using the guard's sword arm to engage in a duel with the second guard.

He shoved both guards out of the way and freed his whip. In a flash, he cracked it around one of the guard's wrists, yanking the sword from his hand.

He swiftly turned the sword in his hand, studying it quickly. He had never used a weapon quite like this one before and was unsure of how best to wield it. Judging from his attackers, he figured that shouting wildly was part of the overall technique, so he let out a savage cry and charged after the guards with his new sword and his trusty whip.

He stopped short, though, when his charge brought him face-to-face with eight more Thuggee guards. His only chance was to retreat — and the only place to retreat to was the rope bridge.

Willie and Short Round were nearly at the other side. He wasn't sure if he could move fast enough to catch up with them, but he would try. He just hoped the guards would be too intimidated by the bridge's scary sway and unsafe appearance to follow him. After all, if they all charged out onto it, the whole thing might come down.

Still gripping his whip and the sword, he headed out, walking as quickly as possible across the rickety span. He kept his eyes down, judging the safety of each board until he became suddenly aware of shouting ahead of him.

Looking up sharply, he saw ten Thuggee guards and Mola Ram waiting on the far side of the bridge. Willie and Short Round were so intent on watching their every footstep that they were taken by surprise when they reached the end of the bridge and were seized by the guards.

He watched helplessly, swaying in the middle of the bridge with Mola Ram in front of him, Thuggee guards behind, nothing but the sky above, and the rocky river gorge filled with hungry crocodiles below. Wind whipped around Indy and he staggered unsteadily. "Let them go, Mola Ram!" he shouted over the howling wind.

Even from a distance, he could make out Mola Ram's diabolical sneer. "You are in a position unsuitable for giving orders," he jeered.

"Watch your back!" Willie suddenly warned urgently as she struggled in vain to free herself from her captors.

Whirling around to where he'd just been, Indy saw Thuggee guards starting across the bridge toward him.

He was utterly trapped.

It was time for a serious negotiation with Mola Ram.

He pulled the pouch of Sankara Stones from his satchel and dangled it over the gorge. "You want the stones?" he shouted. "Let them go!"

Mola Ram was unflustered, even amused by this. "Drop them, Dr. Jones," he replied with a nasty smile. "They will be found in the gorge. You won't."

"Indy!" Short Round shouted in alarm, twisting and struggling in a guard's iron grip.

"Behind you!" Willie cried out.

Mola Ram shouted a command in his ancient language and the guards closed in on Indy from both sides.

His eyes darting in both directions, Indy looped the pouch of stones around his neck and considered his predicament, muttering a curse under his breath. He was certain he'd been in worse situations than this one — but at the moment he couldn't think of any.

The guards crept closer still, brandishing their swords.

Desperate times called for desperate measures, he thought, as a plan formed in his mind.

He lifted the sword, threatening to bring it down on the bridge's rope handrail.

Mola Ram's smile faded slightly. With his dagger, he gestured for Willie and Short Round to move out onto the bridge. The guard's released them but they hesitated, not sure what his intentions were. "Go on! Go!" he demanded impatiently.

Reluctantly, Willie stepped out onto the bridge.

"Go on!" Mola Ram snapped, shoving Short Round forward. "Go on! Get going!"

Indy watched intently as Short Round followed Willie onto the bridge. "Shorty!" he shouted to get the boy's attention before switching to Chinese so no one but Short Round would know what he had in mind.

As Indy spoke to Short Round rapidly in Chinese, he carefully hooked his own leg around the webbing of the side spans of the bridge.

Short Round's face took on an expression of sheer terror but he nodded and hooked his arm into a rope stay.

Indy glanced at Willie with a meaningful expression

and a nearly imperceptible nod that said: *See what we're doing? Do the same.*

As the realization of what Indy was about to do struck Willie, she staggered back two steps. "He can't be serious!" she muttered frantically.

"Hang on, lady," Short Round told her. "We're going for a ride."

Moving rapidly, Willie wrapped a piece of frayed rope securely around her arm and squeezed her eyes shut. "Is he nuts?" she asked Short Round as Indy raised the sword over his head once more.

"He no nuts. He crazy," Short Round replied.

With the sword still poised over his head, Indy looked Mola Ram straight in the eyes and swung the sword with all his strength. It whooshed through the air and slashed clear through the top and bottom ropes!

Immediately, Mola Ram's guards started to flee in panic — but it was too late! The rope bridge was shorn in two! As it broke in the middle, both halves swung down toward opposite sides of the gorge.

The guards shrieked horribly in mid air as they fell from the bridge and hurtled toward the croc-infested river. Mola Ram pitched forward, off balance, as he clutched at the bridge's ropes and slats.

Willie and Short Round clung to the ropes they had wrapped around themselves. They fell with the bridge toward one of the cliff walls. Below them, Indy stayed latched onto his rope support and also swung with the bridge as it hit the sheer face of the cliff wall.

The bridge now hung like a ladder, with Short Round and Willie closer to the top and Indy hanging on below. But above them, Mola Ram also dangled, along with one of his guards.

Mola Ram tried to climb upward, but a slat broke in his hand. "Noooo!" he shrieked as he lost his grip and plummeted past Willie and Short Round. Flailing wildly, he managed to grab onto the rope once again, knocking another of his guards down into the gorge.

He wasn't far below Indy now, and began to climb up. The Thuggee High Priest was surprisingly strong and agile. He quickly reached Indy and was about to pass him when Indy reached out and grabbed his leg. Indy wasn't going to let Mola Ram climb and reach Willie and Short Round before they could escape to the top.

Mola Ram kicked violently, trying to break Indy's grip on his leg but Indy was determined not to let go. He yanked Mola Ram down the rope until they were face-to-face. Mola Ram stretched toward Indy, trying to reach his chest.

"Indy, cover your heart!" Short Round warned from above. "Cover your heart!"

Indy remembered what Mola Ram had done to the

sacrificial victim in the temple. He writhed away from the High Priest, more terrified than he had been even when he cut the rope bridge in two.

Still clinging to the vertical rope bridge, Mola Ram's fingers inched toward Indy's chest. Indy clutched Mola Ram's wrist, trying to keep the deadly fingers away from his heart. The High Priest simply laughed and began chanting, moving his hand ever closer.

Indiana heard Willie crying out to him from the edge of the cliff.

Slowly, using great concentration to focus all his strength into his arms, he pushed Mola Ram's hand away. But as Mola Ram withdrew his hand, he hit Indy in the face with a powerful blow to the jaw.

Indy lost his grip on the rope.

He was falling!

Reaching out as he tumbled down, Indy could see the shining triangular teeth of the crocodile below him as he hung no more than five feet above the bottom of the gorge. At the last second, he had been able to grab the rope bridge before plunging into the gorge. His heart hammered in his chest as he dangled there. When its frenetic beat slowed, he pulled himself up and began to climb.

He'd advanced only several rungs when something flew past his face and bounced off the cliff wall. He continued to climb, but an arrow splintered the wooden slat he had gripped. Looking up, he saw that more Thuggee guards had arrived on both sides of the cliff. They stood at each edge and were shooting arrows at him from large bows.

Indy heard shouting from above. "Look out!" Short Round shouted down to Willie.

"Noooo!" Willie wailed as Mola Ram climbed up below her. She kicked at him and pounded on his head, trying to keep him from reaching her.

Mola Ram lost his grip and fell once again. He reached out for Indy as he hurtled past, his fingers grabbing Indy's shirt.

It took all Indy's strength to keep from being knocked off the bridge by Mola Ram's weight. The High Priest regained his grip on the bridge and reached toward Indy's satchel, trying to get the Sankara Stones away from him. "The stones are mine!" Mola Ram bellowed.

"You betrayed Shiva," Indy countered. Speaking in Sanskrit, he repeated the ancient warning about the power of the stones. As Indy spoke the words, the stones began to glow inside the bag.

Mola Ram grabbed for them and their intense heat scorched his hands.

The stones began to spill out of the bag.

Mola Ram reached out, trying to grab them back.

Indy kept speaking the sacred Sanskrit words. The blazing stones seared Mola Ram's flesh and he screamed in pain, letting go of two stones, which dropped into the gorge. He juggled the third stone, determined not to let it slip from his grasp. But the pain was too much, and the stone fell from his hands. But this time, the stone didn't fall into the gorge. Indy thrust his arm out, deftly catching it in midair.

Thrown off balance by the burning stones, Mola Ram reared backwards. Indy watched him plummet downward until he finally crashed into the water.

The crocodiles arose, instantly eager for the meal that had just dropped in.

Indy was once again climbing toward the top of the cliff and dodging arrows when he saw the young maharajah appear on the cliff. Behind him were Captain Blumburtt and his British troops. The maharajah pointed across the chasm to the Thuggee guards on the opposite side who were still firing arrows at Indy, Willie, and Short Round.

The British took aim with their rifles and fired on the guards. It wasn't long before the Thuggees gave up and retreated into the woods.

Willie and Short Round made it to the top of the cliff first. Still climbing below them, Indy was relieved to see them standing on safe ground.

Every muscle in Indy's body ached with the effort of pulling himself up the last several feet to the top. Slowly, painfully, his face lifted above the edge of the cliff. With joyful expressions, Willie and Short Round gripped his shoulders and pulled him to safety.

Indy rolled on his back to recover for a moment. Then, he reached into the pouch that had once carried the three Sankara Stones and triumphantly lifted the one remaining stone he had managed to save. It was the one that belonged to the villagers.

CHAPTER TWENTY

As Willie, Short Round, and Indy emerged from the jungle and looked down a hillside at the Mayapore village below, they could hardly believe the change; brilliant sunshine now shone on blossoming fruit trees and abundant foliage, and colorful, well-kept homes.

Weary, but happy to be safe once again, the threesome entered the village. They were not alone. Behind them followed a multitude of the village children they had freed from the mines. Indy couldn't wait to see the faces of the villagers when they saw that their most valuable treasure — their children — was being returned to them.

Instantly, villagers came forward to greet them. The children rushed forward into the arms of their parents. Cries of happiness and tears of joy filled the air; there was laughter and crying mixed in a soaring exultation as families were reunited.

The old shaman came toward Indy, followed by the

village elders. The shaman touched his fingers to his forehead and bowed. The three travelers returned the greeting.

"We know you are coming back when life returned to our village," the old shaman said with great emotion. He swept his arms around the village. "Now you can see the magic of the rock you bring back."

The old shaman smiled wisely. Indy took the stone from the bag and handed it to him. "Yes, I understand its power now," he agreed.

The shaman took the stone reverently and bowed once again to Indy, Short Round, and Willie. He joined the elders and they walked to the village's small sacred mound. Kneeling, he replaced the stone in its niche.

Willie turned to Indy. "You could've kept it," she pointed out, her voice filled with admiration for the fact that he had not.

"Ah, what for?" he asked. "They'd just have put it in a museum. It would be just another rock collecting dust."

"But then it would have given you fortune and glory," she reminded him.

He smiled at her slyly. "We might find fortune and glory yet. It's a long way to Delhi."

Willie looked up at him with an expression that asked: *Are you crazy?* "No thanks," she declined firmly. "No more adventures with you, Dr. Jones."

Indy played at being shocked. "Sweetheart, after all the fun we've had together?"

Willie's hands went to her hips. "If you think I'm going to Delhi with you, or anyplace else after all the trouble you've gotten me into — think again, buster!"

Indy didn't really think she would travel to Delhi on her own, but he'd come to learn that despite her outward demeanor, she was tough and brave as they came. She might do anything.

"I'm going home to Missouri," she went on, "where they don't feed you snakes before ripping your heart out and lowering you into hot pits. This is not my idea of a swell time!"

Turning, she walked toward a villager. "Excuse me, sir? I need a guide to Delhi," she requested.

Indy suddenly knew he couldn't let her get away. And he didn't believe she *really* wanted to go, either.

Wielding his bullwhip with slow ease, he unfurled it, drew back, and let it out with a flick of his wrist. The whip wrapped around Willie's waist.

Willie frowned angrily as he reeled her in, pulling her toward him and into his arms.

If she had wanted to get away from him, she could have. But she didn't struggle. Instead she gazed up into his eyes and he knew that there was something special between them.

As he bent to kiss her, they were soaked with a spray of water. Jumping apart, they both looked up at Short Round sitting on the back of the baby elephant that had just drenched them and laughing uproariously at his own joke. "Very funny!" he cackled hilariously. "Very funny!"

Indy laughed along and so did Willie. Finally, they kissed — a sign that while one adventure had come to an end, more were waiting on the horizon.